Only You

Rachel Lacey

This is a work of fiction. Names, characters, places, and incidents are either products of the writer's imagination or are used fictitiously and are not to be construed as real. Any resemblance to actual events, locales, organizations, or persons, living or dead, is entirely coincidental.

Only You

ISBN-13: 978-1543192919
ISBN-10: 1543192912

NYLA Publishing
350 7th Avenue, Suite 2003, NY 10001, New York.
http://www.nyliterary.com

Dedication

To my #girlswritenight ladies: Annie Rains, Sidney Halston, Tif Marcelo, and April Hunt. I'm not sure how I ever plotted a book without you!

Acknowledgements

There are so many people who played a part in the making of this little book. First, thank you to my family for helping me find time to squeeze an extra project into my already busy schedule. I appreciate your help and support so much!

To my amazing and tireless agent, Sarah Younger - thank you so much for helping me make *Only You* a reality. I had an idea to write a novella, and you made it happen. I can't say enough how much I love working with you and NYLA. Big thanks as well to Natanya Wheeler for designing my beautiful cover and so much more. Thank you for making my first independent release such a positive experience.

A special shout-out to all my friends in the romance community. When I decided to pursue this crazy dream of becoming an author, I had no idea what an amazing group of people I would be joining. I feel so lucky because I've made so many great friends along the way! You guys are awesome. I'm not even going to try to name names because there are just too many of you, but just know that I love and appreciate you all!

Thank you to my awesome sister, Juliana, and my awesome critique partner, Annie Rains, for beta reading this novella for me. You ladies rock! Also thank you to Will Goodwin for serving as my medical expert (yet again!)

And of course, to my readers - thank you so much for taking a chance on me. I am so grateful for each and every one of you!

One

"Please, Mom? Can't we keep him?"

Amy Jameson tugged at the leash in her hand, nudging the white fluff-ball of a dog her son was currently smitten with further down the aisle of Perry's Pet Boutique. *Can't we keep him?* Dreaded words to a dog-allergic, overworked single mom. "Honey, you know we can't. We're only fostering him until he finds a new family."

Noah sighed, reaching down to pet Yoda, the poodle mix.

Surprisingly, the dog didn't bother Amy's allergies as much as she'd expected. And as of last week, she and Noah had a house of their own to call home, a house that leaned more toward money pit than fixer-upper. But it was hers. And it had a yard, a safe place for Noah to play outside.

Her "no pets allowed in the apartment complex" argument was no longer valid. So how did she explain to her son that she just plain couldn't handle the responsibility, or the expense, of another mouth to feed?

"He needs treats," Noah said, his voice little more than a whisper. "And a bone to chew. And toys."

"Aunt Merry sent over plenty of toys and goodies when we agreed to foster him for her. He just needs a bag of dog food."

"But I really like this one." Noah picked up a chew toy, running his hand back and forth over the raised rubber bumps ridging its surface.

She drew a deep breath, ready to tell him why Yoda didn't need another chew toy, why the half-chewed up thing Merry had sent over with him was totally fine, but she was so tired of saying no. How much could a little chew toy really cost? She reached out and flipped over the tag. $11.99.

Holy crap.

She could pay for Noah's school lunch for a week with that money. "He doesn't need it. Aunt Merry sent plenty of toys for him."

Noah was silent, still rubbing his hand over the rubber nubs on the toy, but she saw the frustration in his eyes. He was tired of hand-me-downs, both for himself and for the mutt sniffing the aisle ahead of them—already a hand-me-down himself as he'd been given up by his first owners, landing him in the animal rescue run by Amy's brother's fiancée until he found a permanent home.

Which would not be with Amy and Noah. She could barely afford to feed the two of them. "I'm sorry, bud."

He put the toy back onto the shelf and walked ahead of her, turning the corner to the next aisle. Always so quiet when he was upset. Just once, she wanted to be able to say yes to what he'd asked for, to see his eyes light up with excitement, to hear him squeal with joy the way he so rarely did.

"Someday," she muttered.

Yoda yanked at the leash in her hand, and she glanced down to see him raise his rear leg in the direction of a pile of rope toys.

"Yoda, no!" She bent and grabbed him around his scrawny ribs, but it was too late. A stream of urine shot out from him, going everywhere. She stumbled forward with a squeak, giving the dog a small shake to get him to quit peeing, and her head bumped into something—or someone.

She turned her head and found herself eye level with a man's crotch. And *oh God,* she had just head-butted him in the groin. She lurched upright, sending a stream of Yoda pee all over the poor guy's pants in the process. "Oh my God. I'm so sorry—"

"Amy?"

That voice. It sent a bolt of longing through her so intense that her whole body sizzled with it. She looked up and into the slightly amused eyes of Luke Benson.

Yoda slipped through her fingers, leaping to the floor to finish his interrupted business.

Luke.

If it was possible, he looked even better than she remembered. The cocky, lean teenager who'd stolen her heart at the tender age of sixteen had matured into a tall, solid man who filled out his worn jeans and T-shirt with a lot more muscle than he'd had in high school. His brown hair was shorter now, close-cut, but his eyes were the same: hazel flecked with a million different shades of green, gold, and brown.

She cleared her throat while her heart pounded against her ribs and her cheeks grew suspiciously warm. "Luke. You're back in town."

"I am." And he was looking at her the way he had in high school, a way no man had since: like she was the most beautiful woman in the room.

Or, in this case, the pet store.

And, oh God, there was a streak of dog pee on the front of his pants. She pressed a hand to her mouth. "I am so sorry about that."

He glanced down at himself and chuckled. "I've had worse."

Right. Because he was a hot-shot doctor now. Divorced and living in Baltimore the last she'd heard. Not that she'd kept tabs on him since they broke up fifteen years ago, because okay, she totally had. "He's—" She looked down at Yoda, who'd finished relieving himself and was once again busy sniffing his way down the aisle. "He's not really mine, or particularly well-behaved."

"I can see that. You look good, Amy. How have you been?"

She rubbed her hands over the front of her threadbare cotton skirt. *Tired. Lonely.* "I'm good. And you—what brings you back to Dogwood?"

"Joe and Amanda's wedding," he said.

Of course. Joe Royce had been a close friend of Luke's in high school. Which was just super because Amy would be at that wedding too. In fact, she was one of Amanda's bridesmaids. She was going solo, of course, and if she had to sit there all night and try not to feel jealous of Luke and his date, she might lose it.

"I'm a stand-in groomsman," he said, a hint of humor in those hazel eyes.

"A what?"

"Eddie deployed a few months ago, and apparently Amanda wanted to keep the bridal party even, so they asked me to step in."

"Oh." Right. She'd heard that Joe's friend Eddie had deployed, but she was certain Amanda hadn't mentioned anything about asking Luke to join the bridal party in his place. "Well, I'm glad it worked out. I know Amanda has been stressing over all the details lately."

He nodded. "I just got back into the states after putting in some time with Doctors Without Borders and didn't have a new apartment in Baltimore yet so I decided to come visit Mom for a few weeks before the wedding."

"That's nice. How is your mom these days?" Amy had always adored Mrs. Benson. She reminded her a lot of her own mom: warm, caring, and funny. And fiercely protective of her only son.

His gaze softened. "She's great. Still up to no good. You know how she is."

Amy laughed softly. "Remember how she busted us that time when you snuck out after your curfew, and I came and picked you up?"

"Yeah." He smiled, and his eyes heated.

Yeah. They'd had sex on the backseat of her Ford Focus that night too.

"Mom?" Noah's small voice pulled her back to the present. He stood at the end of the aisle, a bag of dog food in his arms.

Luke's brow wrinkled as he glanced over his shoulder in Noah's direction. Yep, that's right. She had a kid now. A kid who came before anything else in her life, especially men. Probably Luke would say an awkward goodbye and be on his way.

Which was for the best really.

"Hi there," Luke said instead. "What's your name?"

Noah looked away quickly, rocking from side to side as he clutched the bag of dog food.

"Noah," Amy said quietly. "His name is Noah."

And he's autistic.

And no doubt Luke was mentally calculating the swiftest escape route, much as Noah's father had done. Squaring her shoulders, Amy walked toward her son, dragging the ill-behaved poodle mix behind her.

* * *

Luke Benson eyed the rows of dog food in front of him, but it was all he could do not to stare at the woman beside him. *Damn.* If possible, she was even more gorgeous than she'd been in high school, tall and slender yet curvy in all the right places. Her brown hair had light streaks that might have come from the salon, but he suspected she'd gotten them the old-fashioned way: spending time outside.

He imagined her at her parents' farm, riding horses with Noah. Yeah. She'd always been fun and adventurous; never afraid to get her hands dirty. And after all these years, she still made his heart beat too fast.

He glanced at the boy. Probably eight or nine, scrawny as Luke himself had been at that age, with a shock of brown hair and round glasses that gave him a bit of a Harry Potter look. "My name's Luke. I'm an old friend of your mom's. I'm here to buy dog food too."

"You have a dog?" Amy asked as she walked to her son and lifted the bag of dog food from his arms. He tucked himself in behind her, his hands fluttering restlessly at his sides.

Autistic, maybe. Luke kept his eyes on the shelves in front of him to keep from making the boy any more anxious. "It's my mom's dog. I offered to pick up some food for her, but I had no idea there were so many choices."

"This kind has blueberries, and fruit is good for you," Noah said quietly.

"That's a good point," Luke said, picking up a bag of the food Noah was pointing at. "I bet Dove–that's my mom's dog–would like blueberries."

"They're good for you," Noah said again.

"I'm sold." Luke tucked the bag of dog food under his arm. "Does your dog like the blueberry kind?"

Noah nodded, picking at a loose thread on his shirtsleeve.

"He's not ours," Amy said. "We're just keeping him a little while for T.J. and his fiancée while they look for a permanent home for him."

He let himself glance at her again, and damn if just the sight of her didn't leave him as breathless as if he'd just finished a five-mile run. "How is your brother?"

"He's doing really well." Amy shifted the bag of dog food in her arms.

Noah crouched in the aisle to pet the dog. "Mom?"

"Yeah, bud?"

"If Mr. Luke is a friend of yours, maybe he could fix our air conditioner."

"Mr. Luke is a doctor. He fixes people, not air conditioners, and I told you I can fix it myself. I watched a YouTube video." She glanced at Luke. "We just moved into a new house, and it's kind of a fixer-upper."

Luke knew an opportunity when he saw one, because he'd never been satisfied with the way things ended between them back in high school. He wasn't letting Amy walk out of his life a second time until he was damn sure this thing between them was finished, and, right now, it sure didn't feel finished. "Well, as it happens, I'm pretty good with my hands."

Amy blushed. "Thanks for the offer, but I can take care of it myself."

Suddenly, it didn't feel like they were talking about air conditioners. Luke cleared his throat and dragged his mind out of the gutter because they were standing in the middle of the pet store with a misbehaving mutt and Amy's son as an audience. "I'm happy to take a look. I'm here all week just hanging out with my mom, and I think she's already getting sick of me."

Amy took a step backward. "Thanks, but I already have someone scheduled to come by tomorrow if I can't fix it today."

He shrugged. "If you're sure."

"I am. Well, we should be going. I need to let someone know about that—" She gestured to the yellow puddle on the floor, "and get this guy out of here before he makes any more messes."

"Right. So, I'll see you at the wedding?"

She nodded.

"Excellent." Suddenly this wedding felt like something to look forward to because he absolutely wanted to see Amy again. As she hurried toward the checkout counter, with Noah and the dog following behind her, even the wedding seemed too long to wait.

* * *

Amy kicked the busted air conditioner. "Dammit."

She clutched her toe. Kicking the air conditioner while wearing flip flops was not her brightest idea. But *damn*, this house was a money pit. The night around her hummed with insects. And it was hot. Miserably hot. It was only mid-May, but summer temperatures had arrived early in Dogwood, North Carolina. Amy brushed back a damp lock of hair from her face. So far, homeownership had not been the dream come true she'd been hoping for.

After her grandfather passed away a few months ago, the house had been left to Amy and her brother. Since T.J. already owned his own farm, this little house had fallen into her lap. And it was perfect for her and Noah, if it didn't fall down on its foundation around them. The window screens were full of holes, which she and Noah had spent most of the afternoon patching with construction paper so that they could at least keep the windows open without serving as a buffet for all the hungry mosquitoes in the area.

The carpets were worn and stained. The faucet in the guest bathroom didn't work. And there was a suspicious soft spot under the linoleum in front of the refrigerator that made her fear she'd fall through the floor every time she got a cold drink.

But it was *hers*. And despite its many problems, the house sat on some seriously amazing land. Acres of woods, even a stream for Noah to play in and have boyish adventures until his heart was content. Once she'd finished fixing the place up, it was going to be their sanctuary.

In the meantime...

Amy rubbed at her big toe and debated giving the air conditioner one more kick for good measure. The capable chick on YouTube had made it look like a simple fix. Not so much. At least her failure would make a great entry on *Everyday Emmy*.

Yeah, her friends and family had no idea she moonlighted as a blogger and was making enough money at it that she'd been able to give up waitressing nights and move to a morning schedule. It meant fewer tips, but so much more time with her son.

Amy was the opposite of most successful "mommy bloggers." She shared real-life experiences that were definitely *not* Pinterest-worthy. She shared her struggles as a single mom and as the mother of a high-functioning autistic son. She told humorous stories about failed do-it-herself attempts like tonight's air conditioning fiasco. And she got honest about the hardships she faced in a way she seldom did with anyone who knew her in real life.

She called herself Emmy, and Noah "Bud," her real-life nickname for him. And somehow her little blog had started bringing in enough ad money that she'd dared to take a leap of faith and move into this house. She was dreaming big for once, terrified of crashing and burning but determined to make life better for herself and her son.

Rubbing at a fresh mosquito bite on her elbow, she tromped inside. Yoda nipped at her heels as she walked to the kitchen for a cold glass of water. He looked up at her, panting.

"Yeah, it's hot in here. I know." She bent and rubbed his fluffy head. Poor dog. He must be roasting under all that fur.

"Want a haircut?" She was joking when the words left her mouth, but why not? She had a set of hair clippers she used to trim around Noah's neck after she cut his hair. Same principle, right?

Yoda cocked his head. Now that she thought about it, Merry had mentioned something about him being overdue to be groomed. "Come on, then. Let's give it a try."

She brought her cell phone with her to the bathroom to take pictures, giggling as she mentally started composing her next *Everyday Emmy* post. A poodle trimming, and a busted air conditioner. Maybe she could even mention his earlier pee-geyser at the pet store.

Two hours later—and with a somewhat-evenly shaved poodle at her side—Amy hit "publish" on her post titled "Fluff and Stuff."

And then, exhausted, she went to bed. As she lay tossing and turning in the hot, humid air, she tried very hard not to think about Luke Benson. He'd been her first real crush. Her first boyfriend. Her first everything.

And they'd been *so good* together. So much in love.

For one perfect year, they'd been inseparable. But Luke was older, a year ahead of her in school so when he got accepted into the pre-med program at Johns Hopkins in Baltimore, Amy tried to be a realist. He'd be living five hours away, a college student in a big city. And Amy, well, she'd just be the small town high school girl from back home.

She knew how these things ended. Rather than waiting around for him to break her heart, she'd done the sensible thing and broken up with him before he left for college.

Except it hadn't been sensible. She'd been miserable without him, and she'd hoped—foolishly—that he'd been miserable without her too. So, she'd scraped together her courage and gone after him, but Luke—looking ridiculously cool and mature on his college campus—had told her it was too late. When he returned home the following summer, he brought his fiancée, Georgia, with him.

A *fiancée*. At nineteen.

Amy's heart was broken all over again. He'd so willingly walked away from her to sow his wild oats in the big city, only to get engaged a few months later? Everyone speculated that he must have gotten Georgia pregnant, but no news of a baby ever came. And Luke married Georgia the following summer, staying in Baltimore with her after he graduated from medical school.

Amy hadn't been much of a believer in love and marriage after that. She and Daryl had been dating for two years when she got pregnant with Noah. And so she hadn't married him, which in the end only made it that much easier for him to leave after their son was diagnosed with autism.

No strings. No looking back.

No more men in her life. Period.

Noah was her priority now. She saw him onto the bus the next morning before hurrying to her shift at the Dogwood Diner. The pay at the diner was less than she'd made at her old job at Finnegan's Irish Pub, but her hours more closely matched Noah's school schedule, allowing her to spend so much more time with her son, and, for the time being, her income from the blog was covering the difference with even a little bit to spare.

Her friend Amanda texted her at lunchtime. *OMG total wedding disaster. There may not even *be* a wedding. Call me.*

Amy shook her head in disbelief. What in the world? Her friend wasn't prone to dramatics. In fact, this had been the most drama-free wedding Amy had ever been a part of. *What happened?* she responded. *I'll be home from work at 2.*

Amanda was waiting in her driveway when she got home, eyes red and puffy. "You'll never believe what's happened."

Amy motioned for Amanda to follow her inside, only to be assaulted by a wall of impenetrable heat inside the house.

"Holy cow," Amanda said, waving a hand in front of her face.

"I know. My AC is busted. I've got someone coming later today to look at it. Let's take some iced tea out on the back patio." Amy ushered Amanda into the kitchen, where she poured two glasses of tea—carefully avoiding the soft spot in the linoleum lest the ground open up and swallow her whole—then led the way out back. "Is it Joe? Did he...?"

Amanda's eyes rounded. "Oh God, no! Nothing like that."

Amy exhaled in relief as she plopped into a chair. "Okay then. Tell me everything."

Amanda sat in the rocking chair beside her. "The country club called this morning. A pipe burst, and there was all kinds of water damage. They're closed for at least a month."

"Oh, crap." This was lousy news, but so much less horrible than the things Amy had been imagining since she'd gotten Amanda's text. No one had died, or cheated, or had anything horrible happen to them. There would still be a wedding, it just wouldn't be at the country club.

"The wedding is only twelve days away! Any place worth getting married at will have been booked months ago." Amanda sniffled as she gulped from her iced tea.

"It could be tricky," Amy agreed.

"My mom is calling every place in the area today anyway, just in case. We might have to elope, but we can't postpone the wedding." Amanda glanced at Amy. "We found out last week that I'm pregnant."

"Oh my God!" Amy lurched out of her chair to hug her friend. "Congratulations."

"Thanks." Amanda was beaming now. "We quit using birth control last month since we're both in our thirties already. We knew we didn't want to wait long, although I didn't necessarily think it would happen *this* fast. But we've got to tie the knot while I can still wear my dress. It cost a fortune."

Well, at least this explained why her normally level-headed friend was such an emotional wreck this afternoon. "You could elope in Vegas. I've always thought that sounded fun."

Amanda laughed. "It does hold a certain appeal. But we love Dogwood, and we want our friends and family to be here to celebrate with us."

"I wonder if there are any local parks that would let you hold a wedding ceremony?"

"That's a thought." Amanda gazed thoughtfully over the open field behind Amy's little money pit of a house. "Something like your backyard would be perfect."

"My backyard, only better tended." Amy looked at the overgrown field behind her house. It would be beautiful...someday. When she'd had time to tame it.

Amanda tapped her fingers to her lips. "This might sound crazy, but what would you think if we had the wedding here?"

"Here?" Amy choked on a mouthful of tea. "As in, at my house? I don't even have a working air conditioner!"

"Out here." Amanda gestured around them, sounding excited now. "We could put an altar right over there." She pointed toward a spot between two oak trees. "And rent a tent. There's plenty of room out here to host everyone."

"Um." It could work. The grounds behind the house were definitely the best part of the property. "It would mean a *lot* of work. No one has done anything with this land in years."

"I'll call Joe and see what he thinks. If he got all his friends out here to help, they just might be able to pull it off." She paused and turned to Amy, her eyes wide and sincere. "If it's okay with you, of course. This is your house. You've barely moved in, and here I am planning my wedding in your backyard."

"Of course I don't mind. It would be really special to have two of my favorite people get married here. My only concern is pulling this off in twelve days because the inside of the house is barely habitable right now, and the land is gorgeous but totally overgrown."

"Joe's friend Max is a landscaper. If he has time, he could be a huge help. And you'd get a whole bunch of free labor—and hot guys—to help get your new house all fixed up." Amanda smiled.

"I'd definitely need help getting the place ready for an event in less than two weeks." Amy twisted her fingers. "But I didn't agree to this to get free work done on my house."

"Sweetie, I know that." Amanda touched her arm. "But we're getting a full refund from the country club, which means I'm saving oodles of money any way you look at it. I'm imposing on you. The least I can do is make sure my wedding disaster doesn't cost you anything."

Amanda left soon after to talk to Joe and see who they could rally for the project. Amy stood in her living room, trying to swallow down a growing feeling of panic. This place was a total dump inside. How in the world could she ever get it ready for guests in just twelve days?

Her phone pinged with an incoming text. It was from Amanda. *I've got someone coming over to take a look around. Be nice to him.* This was followed by an emoticon with wagging eyebrows.

What in the world was that supposed to mean? Amy was rarely rude to anyone.

Ten minutes later, she heard a knock at her front door. She pulled it open to find Luke Benson standing on the other side, wearing khaki shorts, a blue T-shirt, and a panty-melting smile.

Two

Luke watched surprise flicker across Amy's face. He'd assumed Joe and Amanda would have given her a heads up that he was coming over, but apparently they hadn't. Officially, he was here as a favor for his friends, but unofficially? It was a chance to see Amy again.

"Luke? What are you doing here?"

"Joe told me about the problem at the country club and that they were thinking about having the wedding here. You probably remember my dad's a general contractor."

She nodded, her expression unreadable.

"So I'm pretty good at fixing things up. I offered to come take a look and see if this seems feasible, if it's okay with you?"

"Um, sure. Come in." She stepped back and let the door swing open.

"Thanks." He stepped inside, and the temperature rose at least twenty degrees. "Still no AC?"

She blew a strand of hair back from her face. "The repairman should be here in a few hours."

"Alright." He looked around. The house was small but homey. Amy had filled the living room with cozy touches—photos of Noah and the rest of her family and lots of knickknacks. The gray walls looked recently painted.

"My grandparents used to own this place," she said. "My grandfather lived here alone for the last ten years, and he wasn't in good health so he couldn't keep the place up. It really needs a lot of work. Honestly, I have no idea how I could get it ready in time for the wedding."

"Well, sounds like we'd be outside mostly, although I guess you'd want to be able to have the wedding party get ready in here." He surveyed the rest of the room, taking in the worn carpets and window screens patched with colorful pieces of paper.

Amy stood by a table in the hallway, fiddling with her wireless router.

"Internet not working either?" he asked.

She huffed in irritation. "It went out this morning. This place is testing my last nerve right now."

He fought a smile. "Guess that's one of the joys of inheriting an old house. Mind if I take a look?"

"I guess not. Thanks. It's always been kind of tricky, but usually after I reboot it a few times, I can get it working."

He walked over to the table. "Sometimes I have luck by letting the modem completely reset itself before I plug the wireless router back in."

"It wouldn't be that big of a deal, but Noah has these YouTube videos he likes to watch." She gave him a small smile. "It's this guy who builds things with Legos. Weird, right?"

"I can think of a lot worse things he could be watching."

"Yeah. Well, anyway, it's his routine to watch a video after he finishes his homework in the afternoon, and he has a hard time when his routine gets disrupted." She paused, giving him an assessing look. "He's autistic."

"I figured."

She nodded, looking away.

He restarted the modem, waited a few minutes until it had connected, then plugged the wireless router back in. "Try it now."

Amy walked to a laptop on the kitchen counter and tapped it to life. "It works! Oh my goodness. Thank you."

"No problem." He walked to a corner of the living room where the carpet had peeled away from the wall and lifted it, then pulled it back a little farther. "Looks like you have hardwood floors under here."

"Really?"

"Yep. Shouldn't be hard to rip this carpet right out if you'd like me to. Mind if I take a look outside?"

She shook her head, lingering in the kitchen as he went out the back door. Ah, now he saw why Joe and Amanda wanted to have the wedding here. Behind the house was a big open field rimmed with trees and a stream along the back.

It was wild and overgrown, but Luke didn't see any reason they couldn't have the place ready for the wedding in two weeks. And if it meant he got to spend some extra time here with Amy helping to get the place ready? All the better.

She came out the back door carrying two glasses of what looked to be iced tea. From here, she could be the same Amy he'd fallen head over heels for back in high school. Only as she walked closer could he see the differences. The hesitation in her eyes. The rigid set of her shoulders, as if she carried the weight of the world on them.

The little white dog followed her out the back door and dashed across the open field, chasing a butterfly.

"That the same dog?" he asked, because it was sporting about half as much hair as it'd had yesterday at the pet store.

"Yeah. He needed a haircut to survive the heat in there."

Their fingers brushed as she handed him a glass of iced tea. Amy's face was flushed and glistening from the heat, and he wanted to kiss her something fierce. "Thanks."

She stared across the field at her dog, keeping her gaze everywhere but on him. "You're welcome. Noah will be home from school soon."

"He seems like a great kid."

A soft smile touched her lips. "He is."

"And his father?"

"Out of the picture." Her eyes flashed, and her chin went up.

"I'm sorry."

She shook her head. "I'm not. We're better off without him."

He took a small step toward her. "Well, I am sorry for whatever you and Noah have been through because of him, but I'm not entirely sorry you're single. You are single, right?"

Amy sucked in a breath. Her eyes met his, and she nodded.

He took another step closer. "As it happens, so am I. And I don't know about you, but I never liked the way things ended between us."

He was standing close enough now to see her pulse hammering at her throat, the rapid rise and fall of her chest. Her eyes still locked on his.

"That was a long time ago." Her voice was raspy.

Desire curled hot and strong inside him. "But I still remember exactly how good it was between us."

Her eyes narrowed. "And yet you moved on awfully fast."

Damn. "Amy–"

A diesel engine rumbled from the direction of the road, followed by the squeal of brakes. She pushed past him, headed toward the house. "That's the school bus."

* * *

Amy rushed through the house to the front door, grateful for the distraction but frustrated that Luke was still here as Noah got home. She opened the door and waved at Mr. Nichols, the bus driver, as Noah scampered down the steps and ran toward her. He ran right into her arms for a big hug, and she was never more grateful for the change to her schedule that made it possible for her to be here to greet him as he got off the bus. "Hey, bud. How was school?"

"Whose car is that?" Noah was staring at Luke's SUV.

"Mr. Luke is here. He came to see our house because my friends Amanda and Joe might have their wedding here in our backyard. Doesn't that sound fun?"

Noah didn't answer, still looking at the SUV.

"Mr. Luke also helped fix our internet."

Noah backed out of her arms. "Now I can watch Brick Tricks after I finish my homework."

"Yes, you can." She followed him into the house.

"Hi, Noah," Luke said, a friendly smile on his face. "Did you have a good day at school?"

Noah nodded, eyeing the router in the hallway as he walked toward the kitchen, still wearing his backpack. "The top light's green. That means it's working."

"It seems to be. You want to test it out for me?" Luke asked.

Noah shook his head as he sat at the kitchen table. "I have to do my homework first."

"Ah." Luke met her eyes over Noah's head and winked. "I wish I'd been so studious when I was your age. You must be a smart kid."

Noah unzipped his backpack and pulled out the folder containing tonight's homework. He was one of the smartest kids in his class, but that wasn't why he came straight to the kitchen table after school every day to do his homework. That was just his need for structure and routine.

Any variation from the routine made his anxiety and autistic stimming—the hand flapping and other repetitive movements—worse. Amy opened the back door and angled a fan in Noah's direction to bring in some fresh air. Then she walked to the fridge and poured him a glass of ice water. She set it on the table beside him. "What've you got tonight?"

"Math and spelling words."

"If it's all right with your mom, do you mind if I hang out while you do your homework so that I can see some of that Lego video with you afterward?" Luke asked.

Noah nodded, already hard at work on his first math sheet. Yoda lay sprawled on the floor at his feet.

He took her hand, stroking his thumb across her palm. "I liked everything about our time together except the way it ended."

Her eyes narrowed. "Oh yeah, then why did you get married like five minutes after we broke up?"

Oh, no way was she turning this back on him. "You dumped me, remember? After that, I made some admittedly stupid decisions, but if you hadn't ended things, we'd probably be happily married with a house full of kids right now."

She drew back as if he'd slapped her. "What in the world is that supposed to mean?"

"I was crazy in love with you, Amy. We were good together. I like to think we'd have made it work if you'd given us half a chance."

She pushed past him and walked to the window. "No way. I knew it wouldn't work once you'd gone off to college and left me here, and you more than proved my point."

That struck an uncomfortable chord in his chest. Was she right? Would he have gotten caught up in college life and left her behind? "Then forget about the past and focus on the present. I want you. I'm pretty sure you want me too. Why not see what happens?"

She shook her head. Her jaw was set, but her eyes welled with hurt and regret. "I can't."

He heard the squealing brakes of the school bus outside. The conversation might be over for now, but it wasn't over for good. Not if he had anything to say about it.

Three

Having all manner of hot, sweaty men working in and around her house was proving to be highly distracting. Well, one hot, sweaty man in particular anyway. Amy kept her eyes firmly on the tray of lemonade she carried as she walked onto the back patio. "Who's thirsty?"

They descended on her like ants on a picnic. Joe was first to the patio, his dark skin glistening with sweat under the hot midday sun. "You are the best. You know that, right?"

"If supplying lemonade while you guys sweat your butts off out here makes me the best, then so be it." She smiled sweetly as they all grabbed glasses from the tray she held. It was Saturday—one week until the wedding—and Joe and Amanda had recruited anyone and everyone they knew to help out here today.

Luke lifted the last glass off her tray, looking particularly delicious despite the sweat running down his face. He wore a battered gray T-shirt that showed off some impressive muscles beneath. He took a long drink, his eyes never leaving hers. "Thanks."

"Welcome." Heat bloomed inside her, growing hotter the longer he stared, and yeah, it had been way too long since she'd had sex because she was about to go off like a firecracker just looking at him. She squirmed beneath his gaze.

"Christ." Luke scrubbed a hand over his face. He gave her one last smoldering look, then walked off to join the other guys.

Seven days. Surely she could survive one more week of having him around without jumping his bones like a sex-starved maniac. Okay, the sex-starved part might be true. She'd had one drunken one-night stand after Daryl left her. The sex had been terrible, and the whole encounter left her feeling nothing but sleazy. Since she didn't have time for an actual relationship while raising Noah, she'd come to the conclusion that she'd just have to put her own needs aside for now.

And it had been fine. Until Luke Benson walked back into her life.

Now all she could think about was getting him naked and letting him take care of the restless ache still throbbing inside her. He'd been good at it, even as a teenager.

"You're looking at Luke like you want him naked in your bed."

Amy whirled, her cheeks burning. "What?"

Amanda stood there, a smug smile on her face. "You do! Look at you. Your cheeks are as red as ripe tomatoes."

"I don't." Amy touched her cheeks with her free hand self-consciously. "Well, he's not hard to look at anyway."

"Not at all." Amanda gave him an apprising look before turning her gaze to her husband-to-be. "Although I think Joe's got him beat."

"It's looking great out here," Amy said, changing the subject. "I never would have thought of it myself, but I think it's going to make a really beautiful wedding location."

Amanda's eyes grew misty. "It's gorgeous. The change has been a lot of extra stress, but in the end, it might turn out even more special than the country club."

"Definitely more unique." And it really was special that Joe and Amanda would be married here. Amy watched as Noah planted flowering bushes along the edge of the patio with Amanda's sisters Tara and Becca.

"I found the perfect arbor on eBay," Amanda said. "It's being delivered on Tuesday. And I even rented a couple of those fancy port-a-potties so that we don't overwhelm your plumbing."

Amy nodded with a smile. "That's probably for the best. This house is ancient, and the plumbing is not the most reliable." Although, thanks to Luke, the faucet in the guest bath was working now, and she had gorgeous new—old—hardwood floors in her living room.

She still felt guilty about being on the receiving end of free home improvements because of her friend's wedding, but Amanda assured her everything was being paid for out of her refund from the country club and that she would have spent at least twice as much anywhere else trying to recreate what she could have here at Amy's for virtually free.

Amy walked inside to put the tray away, then she and Amanda joined Noah and her sisters planting bushes. There was lots of laughter and happy chatter as they worked. Amanda and her sisters shared a rapport Amy wasn't familiar with. Her family was close, really close, but she had a brother, not sisters, and it was a totally different dynamic.

T.J. had been more likely to give her an atomic wedgie than share stories and gossip. It made her sad sometimes that Noah wouldn't have a sibling. But he had a loving, supportive family, and that was more than a lot of kids had.

"Mom," he said. "Look."

He held some kind of gross, wiggly bug on his outstretched palm.

"Oh!" Amy tried not to recoil. "Look at that." Boys were so weird. She was convinced she'd never fully understand them.

"Oh my goodness," Becca half-shrieked. "What in the world is that?"

Amanda gagged.

"Looks like some kind of grub," Luke said from behind them.

Amy turned to see him leaning over Noah, his brows drawn in concentration as he studied the bug in her son's hand.

"Cool." Noah set the bug gently back into the dirt, and all the women heaved an audible sigh of relief. "I need to go wash my hands now." He stood and walked off toward the house. Luke walked beside him, still talking about bugs.

Noah had a big grin on his face.

"There are stars in your eyes," Amanda whispered in Amy's ear.

"Will you cut it out?" But she knew it was probably true. Watching Luke with Noah warmed the darkest corners of her heart. No man had ever had such a rapport with him except her brother.

"Need your opinion on something," Luke said to her when he came back out of the house.

"Okay." She stood, wiping dirt off her knees.

He led her across the field to the spot by the two oak trees where the ceremony was to take place. "They want to put the arbor here, which means we'd have chairs set up across the grassy area there." He gestured in front of them. "The tent will go over there, and we'll run power out to it for speakers and fans in case it's as hot next Saturday as it is today."

Amy nodded. "Okay."

"Amanda wants to have that tree cut down." He pointed toward the Dogwood that had been Amy's favorite place to sit and read when she'd visited her grandparents' house as a child. "So that it's not in the way of the tent. I just wanted to check with you first."

Amy looked at the little tree. "Well, I am kind of fond of that tree, but if it's in the way, you can cut it down."

"It's your property. If you want to keep the tree, just say so."

"What I want most is for Amanda to have the wedding of her dreams."

Luke gave her a long look, then his lips curved in a soft smile. "Do you always put everyone else's needs above your own? You like the tree. I'll find a way to save the tree."

"It's just a tree." And what was he talking about anyway?

"It's okay to speak up for what you want, Amy." With a slight shake of his head, he walked away.

* * *

Luke wiped sweat from his eyes and surveyed his work. Not bad. The arbor had gone together easily, and—from his strictly guy standpoint—it looked good. Everything seemed to be on track for the ceremony on Saturday, only four days away now.

Amy came out the back door of the house, looking good enough to eat in a pink summer dress and matching sandals. "That looks perfect."

"Think Amanda will approve?" he asked.

She nodded.

"You could keep it, you know. Put a little bench here or something."

"Might be a nice place to sit and read." A soft smile turned her lips.

"Also a great place for a first kiss as husband and wife." He winked.

Amy's cheeks turned the color of her dress. "Yes."

"I've enjoyed being here this week, with you and Noah." He stepped closer and took her hand.

She looked up at him, worry bunched in her brows.

Yeah, she didn't want him to say what he was about to say, but too damn bad. He was only in town another week unless she gave him a reason to stay, so there was no time to wait for her to come to her senses on her own. "I like you, Amy. So damn much. I'd really like to see if there could be a second chance for us."

Her gaze fell to his chest. "I can't. Not right now."

"Why not now? I'm here. You're here. Who knows when or if that will happen again?"

She looked up, her brown eyes swimming with doubt. "That's exactly the problem. You don't live here, and I don't have time for things that aren't permanent."

"I could live here." He tugged her closer, but she dug her heels in, refusing to fall into his arms.

"But you don't. You live in Baltimore. Your job is there. And I... I really don't have time for anything but Noah right now."

"Those are tomorrow's worries. Right now, you and I are standing together under this wedding arbor, and I really, really want to kiss you."

"You really shouldn't." She stared at his lips.

His blood heated beneath her gaze. "You're all I think about, Amy. Please let me kiss you."

"This is crazy," she whispered. Her eyes closed, and she leaned in ever so slightly.

All the invitation he needed. He bent his head and brushed his lips against hers, lingering there in case she changed her mind. But she stepped closer, sliding one hand cautiously over his chest, making him burn everywhere she touched.

He slid his hands around her waist, anchoring her against him as he kissed her again. This time her lips parted beneath his. His tongue slid against hers, and she let out a breathless moan. They kissed until his heart felt like it might burst out of his chest and he was so turned on his whole body ached with it

"Amy." He drew her closer, sliding his hands down to cup her ass. God, she felt perfect, so perfect, in his arms. "I want you so much."

"I want you too, but that doesn't make it a good idea." She drew back to look into his eyes, gasping for breath, her lips pink and swollen from his kisses.

"Doesn't make it a bad one either." In fact, right now his dick was reminding him that it had been a long, *long* ass time since he'd gotten laid.

"Do you think it would be as good as we remember? I mean, we were just kids." She settled closer in his arms.

"Only one way to find out." He winked playfully, but he knew she wasn't ready.

"Typical man. Is it really all you think about?"

"At this particular moment, yes, all I'm thinking about is sex. Specifically, sex with *you*, Amy Jameson. Even though I know we're not going to, not today anyway."

"No?" Her eyes had gone all hazy, and she pressed her hips against his.

He didn't pull away. "No. For one, I need you to be sure. And two, Noah will be home soon, and if we do this, *when* we do this, I want to be able to take my time with you."

"Oh." She chewed her bottom lip and stared at him.

"But you could kiss me again in the meantime if you want."

Her lips slammed into his almost before the words were out of his mouth. This was no sweet kiss like they'd shared earlier. This one was raw, and fierce, and passionate. She rocked her hips against him as they devoured each other in what might have been the hottest kiss of his life. Without even meaning to, his hands had slipped beneath the fabric of her skirt, palming her ass through the thin, silky material of her panties.

Amy whimpered, and *dammit,* his control was slipping. Maybe it was because it had been almost two years since he'd had sex. Or maybe it was just Amy. Because she was so beautiful and amazing and sexy. Because she'd been his first, and he wanted her to be his last.

"Luke," she panted, sounding every bit as out of control as he was. "Oh—"

The rumble of a diesel engine reached them, followed by the squeal of brakes. Amy leaped out of his arms. She stood there for a moment, gasping for breath, and then she ran for the house.

Luke scrubbed a hand over his face and watched her go.

Four

Amy messed around in the kitchen while Noah did his homework, because *holy crap,* she was still completely flustered by her encounter with Luke under the wedding arbor. She hadn't been that out of control since, well, since Luke left town fifteen years ago.

And that was a scary thought.

The chemistry between them was as explosive as ever. Maybe more so. But what really scared her was that he made her long for other things, more than sex. Love and marriage and happily ever afters that she hadn't wanted since she'd been a teenager in his arms.

She wanted Luke. In every possible way.

"I'm going to go put on Brick Tricks," Noah said. He slid his homework folder into his backpack and headed for the living room. Yoda trotted at his heels, and Amy knew she'd find them curled up on the couch together momentarily. When Noah was home, they were never more than a few steps away from each other. Yoda even slept in his room at night.

Luke passed them in the doorway and walked to the refrigerator to pour himself a glass of ice water. He downed it in several big gulps, then stalked toward her with a sexy smile. He leaned in so that the stubble on his cheek tickled her ear. "We aren't finished."

And then, with a wink, he followed Noah into the living room.

Amy spun to pour her own glass of water, her throat suddenly gone dry. Somehow, in the past week, Luke had gotten into the habit of watching Brick Tricks with Noah every afternoon after he'd finished his homework. Sometimes they'd play Legos together afterward, or Noah would help Luke with whatever he was working on in the house.

This afternoon's task—for Amy at least—was repainting the kitchen. Yesterday, with Luke's help, she'd gotten rid of her grandparents' old, stained rooster wallpaper. Today, she was repainting the room a soft, happy yellow. She hoisted herself up on the counter to resume her task of sticking painter's tape around the edges of the cabinets and ceiling. She'd just finished applying tape when she heard the tune that played at the end of every Brick Tricks episode coming from the living room.

"You want to help me pot some flowers outside while your mom paints?" Luke asked Noah. "It might get stinky in here for a little while."

"It shouldn't take me too long," she said. "There isn't much wall space, and I'll keep all the windows open."

Noah followed Luke out the back door.

Amy pressed a hand to her heart as she watched them working together outside. Noah nodded at something Luke was saying, his little face so serious as he walked to the row of ceramic pots Amanda had brought over last night.

Shaking her head at herself, Amy went down the hall to her bedroom to change into old jean cut-offs and a T-shirt for painting. Back in the kitchen, she pried open the can of yellow paint and got to work. An hour and a half later, the kitchen was finished, and Amy felt like jumping for joy. The kitchen looked so bright, and sunny, and cheerful. She already loved it, and she hadn't even taken the bright blue painter's tape down yet.

Eager to show Noah, she stepped outside. He and Luke were probably getting hungry for supper too. Luckily, she had leftover pizza in the fridge because there was no way she was cooking in the kitchen while the paint was still wet.

"Hey, Noah, wait until you see the kitchen!" she called as she walked toward them.

Noah and Luke had filled all but one of the pots with bright pink flowers and were busily potting the last one, while Yoda lay panting beside them. Noah looked up at her. He jumped to his feet and took off running toward the house, but his feet got all tangled up beneath him and he went down in a heap. His head slammed into one of the ceramic vases he and Luke had just finished filling, sending shards of pottery and dirt everywhere.

That's when everything went into slow motion. Amy heard herself screaming his name, felt her feet pounding across the patio as she ran toward him, tasted the sour tang of panic in her throat.

Noah sat up, his face covered in blood. A high, keening wail tore from his throat. His hands started to flail.

"Oh my God, baby. Where are you hurt?" She dropped to her knees beside him.

He moaned, his eyes glassy. Blood streamed down the right side of his face. His glasses had gotten knocked off, and he looked even younger and more vulnerable without them. He brought his hands to his face, smearing blood everywhere.

"Tell me where it hurts," she said, cautiously touching his chin to get a better look. She was trying not to panic, but there was so much blood, and she'd left her cell phone inside. This might be serious enough for a 911 call. Oh God. *Noah...*

Yoda jumped into his lap and started licking his fingers. Amy pushed him aside, but the little dog didn't go far, pressing himself against Noah's right leg.

Luke knelt in front of them, his hazel eyes intense yet calm. "Amy, run around front and get the black bag that's in the trunk of my car. It's unlocked."

She just stared. "What? But Noah's hurt. I—"

He put a hand on her shoulder. "And I'm a doctor. I'll take good care of him. Now please run and get my bag." He spoke with a quiet authority that broke through the haze in her brain.

Luke was a doctor. Of course he was. *Thank God.*

"I'll be right back, bud. Okay? I'm going to go get Mr. Luke's bag so he can patch you up." She squeezed Noah's hand and took off running around the side of the house. She sprinted to his SUV, swung the rear hatch up, and grabbed the black duffel bag she found inside. Then she ran as fast as she could back to the patio.

But they weren't there.

She hurried to the back door and found Luke and Noah in the living room. Luke had thrown one of the tarps she'd brought out for painting over the couch. Noah lay on it, Yoda clutched in his arms.

Luke glanced over his shoulder at her and put his hand out for the bag. "Thanks. Now could you bring me a couple of cold, wet towels?"

She nodded, breathless. All she really wanted to do was sit with Noah and be sure he was okay. But first she could get some towels. She went into the bathroom and grabbed all the hand towels out of the linen closet. She wet them under the sink, placed them in the big plastic bowl she used when she was cutting Noah's hair, and hurried back to the living room.

"Great," Luke said. "You can use one to clean off his hands while I clean his face."

Noah was staring wide-eyed at his blood-stained hands. He couldn't stand for his hands to be dirty, and he'd never liked the sight of blood. Either Luke knew that cleaning his hands would help calm him, or he was just trying to keep her busy.

Amy pried Yoda from Noah's arms. This was not the time or place for the dog. Noah whimpered, reaching for him. She set him on the floor and started wiping Noah's hands.

"Okay, buddy. This may sting a little, but I need to wipe off your face to get a better look at your cut." Luke touched Noah's shoulder, then took one of the hand towels and gently began wiping blood from his face.

Noah started to wail again, that high-pitched noise he only made when he was really hurt or frightened, like a wild animal in pain. Yoda leaped up onto his chest, and Noah's arms clamped around him.

"Not now, Yoda." Amy scooted the dog back onto the floor. "It's okay, Noah. I'm right here. And Mr. Luke is a really great doctor." At least she hoped so, but he certainly seemed capable. "He's going to get you all fixed up."

Noah wailed louder, his hands flailing. Yoda whined at her feet.

"Let him hold Yoda," Luke said. "He's not in my way."

Well, the damn dog was in *her* way. She couldn't see past him to clean Noah's hands, and it couldn't be sanitary to have a dog so near his wound. But Yoda overruled her, jumping back up. Noah gripped him, his cries silenced, arms still.

And she was an idiot. Yoda helped calm him. Dogs had always had that effect on Noah, this one in particular.

She glanced at the side of Noah's head where Luke was working, and her stomach twisted up in knots. *So much blood.* Had he fractured his skull? "Should I dial 911?" she whispered.

Luke looked over at her with a reassuring smile. "Don't even think about it."

"But–"

He shook his head, looking amused. "It's just a superficial laceration. Scalp wounds bleed a lot. I don't think this one's even going to need stitches. Hear that, Noah?"

But Noah had completely zoned out. He held tight to Yoda, his eyes glassy and unfocused.

"He spent a few days in the hospital last summer with a concussion," she told Luke. It had been terrifying for all of them but especially for Noah.

Luke just nodded. He reached into the bowl and pulled out a fresh towel. "Okay, Noah, I'm going to put some pressure on your cut now to get the bleeding to stop. It might hurt a little at first so I need you to do something for me. Okay?"

Noah nodded slightly.

"Good boy." Luke patted his shoulder. "I want you to close your eyes now and start replaying that last episode of Brick Tricks in your head."

Noah whimpered, but his eyes closed.

Luke pressed a clean towel against the side of his head. Noah yelped.

"Should I get him some ibuprofen?" she asked.

Luke shook his head. "That could increase his bleeding. You okay, Noah?"

Noah didn't respond, but he didn't cry either.

"Remember how they took all those red and white bricks and built that cool lighthouse?" Luke said. "I really liked how they alternated the colors like that. It made a nice pattern."

Amy squeezed Noah's hand. Legos. Patterns. How did Luke already understand her son so well? Right now, he was doing a better job than she was at keeping Noah calm.

Noah lay with his eyes closed, still holding onto Yoda. The little dog just lay there, panting, looking completely content. They sat like that for what felt like a long time, while Luke talked about Brick Tricks and held the towel firmly against the side of Noah's head. Noah lay still and quiet the whole time.

"Okay," Luke said finally. "I'm going to have another look at your cut now."

He lifted the towel, and, to Amy's amazement, there was nothing left but a thin, red line along Noah's hairline where his head had hit the planter. It didn't look bad at all now. Amy felt the knot in her stomach ease for the first time since he'd fallen.

Noah's eyes popped open. "It hurts."

"I know it does, bud. I'm so sorry." She squeezed his hand.

"Let me finish fixing up your cut, and then your mom can get you an ice pack." Luke reached into his bag and took out a small light. He felt along the cut on Noah's head, tugging gently at the edges. "Good news. No stitches. Now I just need to check and make sure you don't have another concussion."

"It doesn't feel like it did in my brain the last time," Noah said quietly.

"Well, you are a really smart boy to be able to feel the difference like that," Luke told him. "And I think you're right, but I just need to be sure. I'm going to shine a light in your eyes now. It won't hurt, so try not to blink, okay?"

He checked Noah's eyes, then asked, "Do you see any funny spots when you close your eyes?"

Noah shook his head.

"Any funny noises in your ears, like a bug buzzing around you?"

Another shake.

"And how bad does your head hurt right now, like kind of sore or super, duper painful?"

"It just hurts where the cut is."

Luke nodded. "That's good. Do you remember what we were doing right before you fell?"

"Potting flowers," Noah said, his voice little more than a whisper.

"What did I ask your mom to get out of my car?" Luke asked.

"Your black bag. It was in the trunk."

"Great memory, Noah. I just need you to do a couple more things for me to make sure your brain's a-okay in there. Can you count backward from one hundred by sevens?"

A small smile creased Noah's face. "Easy. One hundred, ninety-three, eighty-six..." He kept going, his voice getting stronger with each number. Amy gave his hand a reassuring squeeze. Noah had always excelled at math. He liked order, and numbers, and patterns.

"Awesome job, Noah," Luke said when he'd finished. "I'm going to ask you to take my hand and sit up now. Let me know if the pain in your head gets worse or if you start to feel dizzy at all."

Amy lifted Yoda out of his arms and set him on the floor. Then Noah gripped Luke's hand and sat up. He whimpered, his hand automatically going for the cut. Luke intercepted him gently, folding his hand back into his lap. "I know it's hard, but try not to touch it. In a minute, I'm going to disinfect it and put a bandage on there to keep it clean, okay?"

Noah nodded, his little face pinched and miserable.

Luke asked him to stand with his feet together, arms extended palms up, eyes closed, and count backward from ten. While Noah counted, Luke stood with his arms out, ready to catch him if he fell. "Great job," he said when Noah had finished. "You can sit down now and relax. And, Amy, you can go get him that ice pack."

"Really? So you're not worried about a concussion?"

He shook his head. "Nah. I don't even see any bruising around the wound. Keep an eye on him tonight in case any new symptoms develop, but I don't see any signs of a concussion."

"Are you sure?"

Luke put his hand on her shoulder. "He didn't lose consciousness. His balance, memory, and cognitive function are not impaired, and his pupils are equal, round, and reactive to light just like they should be. So yes, I'm sure."

"Sorry." She pressed a hand over her eyes. "You're a doctor. I'm being ridiculous."

"No, you're not. You're being his mom. Now be glad I was here and saved you an ER visit and go get him an ice pack for his sore head." There wasn't the least bit of annoyance in his voice.

She nodded and went into the kitchen, tears suddenly pricking the backs of her eyes. *Noah was okay.* He didn't even need stitches. She gulped a deep breath and tried not to totally lose it.

Get it together, Amy.

Her hands shook as she took a cold pack from the freezer, wrapped it in a paper towel, and walked back to the couch. She handed it to Noah, then pulled him in and hugged him tight. His arms wrapped around her, his face tucked against her neck like he'd done when he was little. He might be nine now, but when he was hurting, he was still her baby. And right now he seemed like he needed this hug every bit as much as she did.

When she finally pulled back, she saw a streak of blood across his cheek. "Oh, no. I made it bleed again."

"It's likely to bleed on and off a little bit right now," Luke said. "I'm going to clean it up and put a bandage on it. Sound okay, Noah?"

He nodded.

While Luke cleaned the wound, Amy walked down the hall to her bedroom. She sat on the bed, pressed her face into her hands, and sobbed.

A few minutes later, she heard Luke's heavy footsteps coming down the hall. "You okay in there?"

"Yeah." She motioned him in. "How's Noah?"

"I told him he'd earned a bonus episode of Brick Tricks, considering the circumstances. Hope that was okay."

She nodded, grateful. "Thanks."

"You okay?" He sat beside her, brushing a lock of hair back from her face.

She sniffed through a smile. "Yeah. Just being an overly emotional mom, I guess."

"No such thing." He slid an arm around her shoulders and tucked her against him. "It's perfectly normal. I see it all the time in the ER. Mom holds it together through all the scary stuff to be brave for her kid, then falls apart after it's all over."

"Really?" She turned her face to him, and dammit she was way too close. Close enough to kiss him.

"Mm hmm." Luke's gaze dropped to her lips, but instead of kissing her, he gave her shoulders a squeeze and tugged her to her feet. "Let's get back to Noah."

She stopped in the doorway of her bedroom. "Thank you. For everything. If you hadn't been here, I probably would have dialed 911 and wasted a whole bunch of money I don't have on ambulance and hospital fees, not to mention traumatizing Noah."

"I'm glad I could help. Would it make you feel better if I stayed here tonight?" he asked. "On the couch," he added after her cheeks grew hot.

No, she definitely couldn't handle having Luke here tonight. "Thanks, but we'll be okay."

He nodded.

Back in the living room, she snuggled in next to Noah and Yoda on the couch, while Luke sat in the chair beside it. They watched two bonus episodes of Brick Tricks, then ate cold pizza.

Noah was nodding off by the time he'd finished his first slice, so she took him down the hall and put him to bed.

Luke was standing in the doorway to the kitchen when she came out. "Sure you're okay?"

"I really am." But dammit, after a million single parenting emergencies, it sure had been nice to have him to lean on this time. "You're really good with him, you know that?"

Luke smiled. "He's a great kid."

He made it sound so simple, but it wasn't. A lot of people were intimidated by Noah's autism. They didn't know how to act around him or treated him like he was handicapped.

She walked into Luke's arms. He felt so warm and solid beneath her palms. "Luke—"

"Shh." He tipped her face up to his. "We definitely have some unfinished business, but not tonight. Tonight, you take care of Noah."

A tear slipped from her eye and trailed over her cheek. She nodded.

"Call me, no matter what time, if you have any concerns or questions. I don't care how silly you think it is, if you're worried, just call. Okay?"

She nodded again. "Thank you."

He kissed her then. Just a quick, gentle kiss that completely melted her from the inside out. "I'll see you tomorrow."

After he left, she stood there for a long time, her mind spinning in a million different directions. She needed to write a post for *Everyday Emmy* tonight, but she was so completely drained she couldn't even bring herself to turn on her laptop.

Instead she went down the hall to her bedroom to wash up and change into her pajamas. Then she tiptoed into Noah's bedroom and curled up in bed beside him. And with his little body safe and snug against hers, she slept.

Five

Other than the bandage on his face, Amy never would have known anything out of the ordinary had happened when Noah woke Wednesday morning. He insisted she swap out the white bandage Luke had applied for a simple Band-Aid so that his glasses fit more easily, and she had to admit, the cut didn't look bad at all in the morning light.

To think so much blood had come from such a small wound.

So she sent him off to school and headed into work and tried not to think about Luke at her house doing whatever he was doing today. He had told her he planned to spend the morning finishing up a few things out back, then he had afternoon plans with his mom. So Amy might not see him until tomorrow.

Which was totally fine.

Even if she was slightly disappointed.

Indeed, Luke had already been and gone by the time she got home from the diner, so she worked in the front yard while she waited for Noah. As usual, he walked straight from the bus to the kitchen table to do his homework. When he'd finished, he shoved everything back into his backpack. "Uncle T.J. wants to take me camping this weekend."

"He does? When did you talk to Uncle T.J.?"

"He called yesterday while you were in the shower. I recognized his number so I answered the phone."

"Oh, okay. Do you want to go camping?" she asked. He'd never gone before, although he stayed over at T.J. and Merry's house often.

"We can go fishing. I like fishing."

"And you're good at it too," she said.

"Mr. Luke will be here this weekend for the wedding, right?" Noah asked.

"Yes, he will. He's good friends with Mr. Joe." Amy wondered what prompted that question. Was Noah tired of having Luke at their house all the time?

"I think Mr. Luke would be a good dad," he said.

She stared at her son. "What makes you say that?"

"I hear other kids at school talking about their dads," he said. "And the ones who like their dads have fun dads that play with them, like Mr. Luke does with me."

She had absolutely no idea what to do with that information. "I'm sure Mr. Luke would be a great dad."

"If you married him, would he be my dad?" Noah looked up at her, making rare eye contact.

She pressed a hand to her chest. "If I got married, that person would be your stepdad. But I don't have any plans to get married, Noah. Mr. Luke and I are just friends."

"I know," Noah said as he got up from the table.

Amy watched as he went into the living room and started queuing up the latest episode of Brick Tricks. What in the world was that about? Was he saying that he wanted her to get married? To Luke? Or was he worried that it might happen? With a sigh, she picked up her cell phone and called her brother.

"You're taking Noah camping this weekend?" she asked when he answered.

He chuckled. "You're welcome."

"What?" She rubbed a hand over her brow.

"Noah asked if he could stay at our place this weekend so that you could focus on the wedding. Camping was my idea, but he seems stoked. We'll just pitch a tent down by the barn in case it's a bust."

Amy glanced at her son, already engrossed in YouTube. Noah had asked to stay with T.J. and Merry this weekend? "Well, that sounds fun."

"Is the Mr. Luke he's been talking about who I think it is?"

Amy grimaced. "Yes, but it's not what you think."

T.J. chuckled. "Well, Noah sure likes him, and he just freed you up to spend the weekend with him, so have fun."

* * *

"You're sure you want to go camping for the whole weekend?" Amy asked Noah on Friday afternoon.

"It will be fun." He picked up his backpack and slipped it over his slim shoulders.

"Well, just call me if you want to come home early. I think you'd have fun here at the wedding too."

There was a knock at the front door, and he ran to answer it. Amy followed.

T.J. stood in the doorway, dressed in his trademark Wranglers and cowboy hat. He smiled at Noah. "You look ready to go."

Noah nodded. "I packed extra clothes in case we get wet while we're fishing."

"Smart thinking." T.J. looked at Amy. "Noah and I are going to have ourselves a great time camping. Good luck hosting the wedding."

"Thanks." Amy pulled Noah in for a hug.

"Bye, Mom." He walked out the front door without a backward glance.

Not for nothing, but he could at least pretend he was going to miss her. "I love you," she called after him. "Have fun. Call if you need anything. T.J., you'll keep an eye on that cut on his head like we talked about?"

Her brother gave her an amused look. "You got it. We'll be fine."

And with that, they piled into T.J.'s truck and left. Amy blew out a breath and headed back inside. Yoda trotted at her heels, shadowing her to the back door. The guys should be here soon to set up chairs for tomorrow's ceremony.

In twenty-four hours, Joe and Amanda would tie the knot, right here in her backyard. It was either ridiculously cool or terrifying, depending on the moment. Right now, it mostly felt terrifying because there was so much still to be done. She needed everything to go smoothly tomorrow. Amanda and Joe had entrusted her with one of the most important days of their lives.

Amy hurried down the hall to change before people started arriving for the rehearsal. Suddenly, the yellow sundress she'd decided on earlier didn't feel dressy enough, and no, she wasn't imagining the look on Luke's face when he saw her. Okay, she totally was.

And she wanted him to get all smoldery looking the way he did when he was about to kiss her, which meant she had officially lost her mind because she did *not* want Luke to kiss her. Well, she did, but it was a bad idea, and she knew better than to go there, and oh goodness, she was working herself into a frenzy over absolutely nothing.

After ransacking her closet, she went with the yellow sundress after all. It was cute and flattering, and dressy enough for a backyard wedding rehearsal. She never fussed over her appearance, so it was ridiculous that she was tonight.

It was all Luke's fault.

Fifteen minutes later, she heard a knock at the door. She smoothed her hands over the front of her dress and went to answer it.

"Ready for us?" Joe asked with a wide smile.

Amy grinned at the sight of him. Joe was an easygoing, happy person in general, but this week and today especially, he looked like the happiest man alive. Luke stood beside him, looking handsome in a blue polo shirt and khaki slacks, and yeah, he had the smoldering thing going on in full effect. She felt herself getting all hot and bothered beneath his gaze.

"I'm ready," she answered Joe, and motioned them inside. The other two groomsmen, Joe's friends Michael and Carlos, followed them in.

The men went through her house and out the back door to start setting up chairs for the rehearsal and tomorrow's ceremony. Amy went with them to help, and also to snap some discreet photos with her phone for a post on *Everyday Emmy*.

Her readers were loving that she of all people was hosting a wedding at her new home this weekend.

"You are killing me in that dress," Luke whispered in her ear.

"What?" She whirled, bumping right into his chest. She backpedaled away from him before anyone noticed.

Luke raised his eyebrows with a sexy grin. He mouthed the word "sexy," and, with a wink, he got back to work setting up chairs.

"Where's Noah?" Joe asked.

"Spending the weekend camping with his uncle."

Luke glanced at her over his shoulder, eyebrows raised. Yeah, she hadn't mentioned it to him yet, mainly because she didn't trust herself once he knew they had the whole weekend to do as they pleased. And from the look on his face, he knew it.

"Oh my God."

Amy spun at the sound of Amanda's voice. Her friend stood beside the house, a hand clasped over her mouth, her eyes already welling with tears. "It's perfect."

Amy walked to her. "It did turn out pretty nice, didn't it?"

It was true. Amy's backyard had transformed from an overgrown field to a beautifully landscaped one. The arbor stood on the left side between two towering oak trees, with rows of white chairs facing it. Tomorrow, it would all be draped in fresh flowers. On the other side of the yard, a tent and tables stood, ready for the reception.

Soon after, Amanda and Joe's families began to arrive, and Amy was swept up in the whirlwind of the rehearsal. She got tears in her eyes watching her friends stand beneath the arbor, knowing that tomorrow they would be husband and wife. Unlike so many couples these days, she had a feeling this marriage would last.

After they'd all practiced their roles for tomorrow, it was time to head into town for dinner. Joe and Amanda had booked a private room upstairs at Torino's, a local Italian restaurant, and their table was soon loaded with food and wine.

"Can I ask you a huge favor?" Amanda whispered.

Amy smiled at her friend. "Anything."

"Would you drink my wine for me?" Amanda gestured toward her untouched glass. "We aren't sharing our news just yet, and I don't want to attract attention tonight."

Amy grinned. "It would be my pleasure." She took a sip of her own wine and set her glass down near enough to Amanda's that she could reach either glass easily. For the next hour, she sipped from both glasses as she stuffed herself on antipasto, bread, lasagna, and tiramisu.

And, because the guys kept topping everyone off, Amy drank a *lot* of wine.

"Tonight has been the best," Amanda said with a dreamy sigh as she plopped her napkin onto her empty plate and gazed at her husband-to-be.

"It has been," Amy agreed. "And you might win an award for most laidback bride ever."

"No kidding," Amanda's sister Becca said. "Losing her venue at the last minute like that? I'd have completely lost it."

"Oh, I did," Amanda said. "But it all turned out great."

Joe's dad made a toast to the bride and groom, and Amy downed the last of her glass of wine while Amanda feigned a sip of her own. People started standing up then, hugging and saying goodnight to the happy couple.

Amy stood cautiously. The room swayed. *Shit.* She'd been able to keep herself together while she was seated, but there was no denying the truth now: she was trashed. Truthfully, she rarely drank more than a single glass of wine, and who knew how much she'd had tonight? Horrified, she just stood there, gripping the back of her chair.

"You alright?" Luke's voice rumbled in her ear, sending warm shivers up and down her spine.

"Mm hmm." She glanced up at him, and *whoa.* Big mistake. She nearly lost her balance and swooned at his feet.

"You look a little bit..." His eyes narrowed. "Amy Jameson, are you *drunk?*"

She sighed. "Possibly."

He grinned at her, looking so damn gorgeous she almost kissed him right there in the middle of the restaurant. His eyes... something about the lighting in Torino's made them even more captivating tonight, swimming with flecks of green and gold. Or maybe that was the wine talking. She kept her white-knuckled grip on the back of her chair.

Luke leaned in close. "You are the cutest—and quietest—drunk I've ever met. Come here." He hooked an arm through hers and led her to a quieter corner of the room near the windows. "Too much wine?" he asked with a wink.

"Not my fault," she muttered, glancing over her shoulder at the group behind them, boisterously saying their good-byes. "I was drinking for two."

Luke's eyebrows shot upward. "Come again?"

She pressed a hand over her eyes. "I'm too drunk to speak coherently. I need to get out of here."

"I'll drive you home."

"Okay." Through her wine-induced haze, that sounded like a *great* idea, because Luke was by far the handsomest man in the room, and it had been almost five years since she'd had sex. If she were honest with herself, he was the only man she'd ever loved. And tonight, who cared about repercussions or the future? Tonight, she just wanted to have sex. She wanted to strip him out of his clothes and find out if he was as good in bed as her memories of teenaged Luke led her to believe.

He gave her a heated look, as if all her thoughts were written all over her face, which they probably were, because she felt her cheeks flush hot. He guided her back toward the table to say their good-byes.

Amy pulled Amanda in for a big hug.

Her friend's eyes widened. "Are you drunk?"

Amy giggled. "Maybe a bit tipsy. It's all your fault."

Amanda blushed. "Shh! Do you need a ride home?"

She shook her head. "Luke's taking me home. I'll see you at my place in the morning to get ready. I'm so happy for you." She pulled Amanda in for another hug.

Amanda laughed. "Me too. Okay, I'll see you tomorrow."

Luke guided her through the door, down the stairs, and outside into the fresh air. Amy drew a deep breath, hoping it might help to clear the fog in her head. No such luck.

"So, drinking for two, huh?" he said as they walked toward his SUV.

"Amanda's pregnant. She asked me to drink her wine for her tonight so no one would notice she wasn't drinking, but everyone kept topping off both of our glasses, and possibly I had a bit too much."

"Possibly." But he was smiling. "That's great news for Joe and Amanda."

Amy nodded. "But shh, because I wasn't supposed to tell."

"My lips are sealed." They reached his SUV, and Luke walked her to the passenger side and opened the door for her.

"Luke–"

"Yeah?" He turned, backlit by the streetlamp behind him.

She leaned forward, fisted her hands in the front of his shirt, and kissed him. He let out a groan that tickled all of her sensitive spots as it rumbled through her, then his tongue swept into her mouth, and he kissed her back. He tasted like red wine and chocolate and the promise of many mind-blowing orgasms.

He pressed her against the side of his SUV, his strong, hard body covering hers, and whoa, was he hard. She felt him pressed against her belly, making her ache for his touch. It had been so long, and she was so turned on right now she couldn't think of anything but getting him out of his clothes and inside her, like *now.*

Luke tore his mouth from hers and gave her a smile that almost sent her right over the edge. "Damn, Amy. Let me get you home."

Right. Because they were still standing in the parking lot of Torino's, and if she weren't so drunk right now, she would definitely be horrified about the fact that she'd just kissed Luke like that out here where anyone could see, especially anyone from the wedding party who might be coming out of the restaurant.

She climbed into the passenger seat and sat quietly while he got in and cranked the engine. The whole inside of the car smelled like Luke, a combination of aftershave and leather that brought to mind many hours spent making out as teenagers. They'd been pretty talented at backseat sex once upon a time. She glanced over her shoulder, eyeing the size of Luke's backseat.

He followed her gaze and laughed. "Don't tempt me."

"I'm tempted," she whispered.

Luke let out a rough sound as he shifted the car into drive and pulled out of the lot. He didn't say anything on the drive to her house, and Amy—well, she just hung onto her seat and tried not to feel sick.

When he pulled into her driveway and shut off the engine, she sat there for a moment in the darkness. "Luke?"

"Yeah?"

"Do you ever wonder what would have happened?" She paused. "You know, if we hadn't broken up?"

"You mean if you hadn't dumped me?" She heard the laughter in his voice. "I told you. I think we'd be happily married with a couple of kids by now."

That's right. He had told her. And as much as she wanted to wish it were true, she couldn't. She wouldn't change a thing, because if she'd stayed with Luke, she wouldn't have Noah.

"Come on." He opened his door and got out of the car.

She opened hers and just about fell on her face in her gravel driveway, which would have been a tragedy the night before Joe and Amanda's wedding. With a chuckle, Luke hooked his arm through hers again and led her to her front door.

"Not sure I've ever seen you this drunk," he said as she fumbled with her key in the front door.

"Shut up." She giggled as she stumbled inside. Yoda came bounding up and sniffed her leg.

"You're an adorable drunk." Luke tugged her in for a kiss, but not the kind of kiss she wanted. This one was quick and chaste, like he had no intention of doing any of the things she wanted to do tonight.

"I'm not *that* drunk," she said.

"Yes, you are."

"Not." She pressed herself into his arms and kissed him back.

He shook his head. "When we do have sex, I need you to be sober enough to remember it."

She grumbled under her breath like Noah sometimes did after she'd told him no.

Luke walked into the kitchen. "In the meantime, you need to start drinking some water."

She grumbled some more as he handed her a glass of water and a couple of ibuprofen and sent her down the hall to change. If she'd had any sexy lingerie, she'd have put it on, but alas, she usually slept in an old, oversized T-shirt.

She sat down on her bed, waiting for the room to stop spinning. This wasn't fun. Her stomach wasn't feeling so great either. Getting drunk had been a lot more exciting when she was younger. She lay back on the bed and closed her eyes, just for a minute.

* * *

When she hadn't come out of her room after fifteen minutes, Luke went down the hall and knocked on her door. It swung open beneath his knuckles to reveal Amy curled up in a cute-as-hell little ball on her bed, fast asleep, still wearing the yellow dress.

Sexy. So fucking sexy.

And not so drunk that he needed to stay here and watch over her tonight. No, it was probably in both of their best interest for him to drive home now. Tomorrow night, though. That was another story.

He went into the kitchen to refill her glass of water and set it on the table beside her bed. He bent to kiss her cheek, then left her there.

At home, he found his mom in the living room watching an old episode of *Law & Order*, with her little dog, Dove, in her lap.

"How was the rehearsal?" she asked, motioning for him to join her.

"Fine, Mom. Everything went well."

"It must be so stressful for Amy, having the wedding at her house. I bet she appreciates all your help," his mom said, not even trying to keep the eagerness from her tone. If there was anyone who regretted the way things between him and Amy ended more than Luke did, it was his mother. "You know, I bumped into her at the supermarket not too long ago. That little boy of hers sure is adorable."

"Yeah, he is."

"I heard he's autistic," she said.

"And you're nosy, Mom. I'm just doing a favor for Joe."

She sighed. "Can't blame a mother for hoping."

Couldn't blame a man for hoping either. He sat with his mom to watch the end of *Law & Order*, letting his mind wander while they figured out who had murdered a bike messenger on the streets of New York. He liked getting to spend this time with his mom. It felt good to be back in Dogwood.

He just might stay, if a certain brunette would give him half a chance at her heart.

He went to bed early and slept like the dead—a handy trick he'd taught himself during years of medical school and overseas with Doctors Without Borders. He woke to the sound of an incoming text message on his phone.

Sorry about last night. It was from Amy.

His dick sprang to attention at the thought of her in bed, all sexy and rumpled from sleep. *No problem. You feeling okay this morning?*

Been better, but I'll live.

Still wearing that yellow dress? Why was he torturing himself? He sucked in a breath as he waited for her answer.

His phone chimed. *No.*

Aw, hell. What he wouldn't give to be in her bed right now.

I just got out of the shower, Amy texted, and the tent in his sheets grew.

Damn, woman.

Do you still sleep in the buff? She added a little winky face to the end of her message.

Boxer briefs. Which were strained to bursting right now. *If you're still wearing your towel, lose it.*

His phone was silent for a long minute.

Okay, she finally answered.

Holy shit. *So you're naked?*

Another long pause. *Yes.*

Damn. Luke blew out a breath. He'd never sent sexy texts with a woman before, certainly wouldn't have imagined himself doing it with Amy. In high school, she'd been so sweet and innocent. She'd have turned beet red if he'd asked her something like, *Are you touching yourself right now?*

In the silence that followed, his mind went to all kinds of dirty places, all of which involved Amy pleasuring herself while he waited here on the other end of the line. He clutched the phone tighter as he waited for her response.

It never came.

He should go take a long, cold shower. Instead, he pressed her number and brought the phone to his ear. "The suspense is killing me," he said when she answered.

"Luke," she sounded breathless...aroused.

And they definitely weren't finished yet. "I'm thinking about you touching yourself right now, and it's hot, Amy. So fucking hot."

She whimpered.

Luke groaned. The images in his head right now were downright X-rated. "Imagine my hands on your body, touching you. I can almost feel how wet you are."

She gasped, and the sound sent a surge of arousal through him. He knew that sound, remembered how she would gasp like that when he was driving her wild with his hands or his tongue. Yeah. She was close.

"I love the way it makes you crazy when I kiss that spot on the side of your neck." His voice had gotten lower, gruff. He squeezed his eyes shut, imagining Amy. Naked. In his bed. "I'm imagining my hands on your body, touching every inch of you until you're screaming with pleasure."

Amy was silent, but he heard a quick intake of breath, so he kept talking, urging her on. He told her all the things he wanted to do with her, how he wanted to taste her, how he wanted to bury himself inside her until they both lost their minds.

There was a pause, and then a soft cry as she found release. Luke fisted his hands in the sheets and gritted his teeth. *Fuck.* That was hot. A shudder rippled through him, settling with a heavy ache in his dick.

"Holy shit," she panted into the phone.

Holy shit indeed.

"I, um, I have to go." With a click, she was gone.

Luke set the phone down and closed his eyes, replaying the soft sounds of Amy's arousal, the way she'd panted his name, her cry as she came...

A knock on his bedroom door nearly sent him careening onto the floor. "Luke?" his mother called. "Are you awake? I'm making breakfast. You need to get a move on before the wedding."

And just like that, his dick shriveled. He cleared his throat, searching for composure. "Let me just hop in the shower, and I'll be right down, Mom."

And what a cold, miserable shower it would be.

Six

Amanda twirled in front of the full length mirror in Amy's bedroom with a radiant smile, then clutched her stomach. "I'm going to be sick." She bustled into the bathroom and slammed the door behind her.

Amy exchanged a glance with Dorothy, Amanda's mother.

"I'll make sure she's okay in there with her dress," Dorothy said and followed Amanda into the bathroom.

Amy walked to the window, smoothing out the floor-length blue chiffon bridesmaid dress she wore. The ceremony started in twenty minutes, and the combination of nerves and pregnancy hormones had done a number on Amanda's stomach.

Amy pushed back the curtains and peeked outside. The backyard bustled with people and happy chatter. Near the arbor, Joe, Michael, Carlos, and Luke stood together in off-white suits with blue shirts that matched the bridesmaid dresses. They each wore a red rose buttoned to their lapel.

They looked handsome, all four of them. Luke stood out from the other three men with his fair skin. Amy had to admit the light-colored suits looked especially dashing on the African American men, but...Luke.

She still couldn't believe what she'd done on the phone with him that morning. She'd been so turned on she'd gotten caught up in the moment, but now...now she was torn between being mortified and still a little bit secretly thrilled that she'd done something so totally unlike herself.

The bathroom door opened, and Amanda stepped out, pale but smiling. "Is it time yet?"

Amy glanced at the clock on her bedside table. "About five minutes. Why don't I go get your dad, and we can start lining everyone up?"

Amanda nodded. Her mom handed her a glass of water, then hustled her back into the bathroom to touch up her lipstick. Amy walked to the living room, where she found Amanda's dad pacing nervously by the back door. "We're ready," she told him.

His eyes lit, and he clapped his hands together. "Finally. Great. Where do you need me?"

"We'll start lining up near the back door." Amy found Becca and Tara in the kitchen, peeking out the window and gossiping about what everyone was wearing. "You guys ready?"

"Yep," Tara said.

"Luke looks hot. Anyone know if he's single?" Becca asked.

"He is," Tara confirmed.

Amy bit her tongue and hoped she looked more nonchalant than she felt.

Becca went to the back door and motioned to the guys to let them know they were ready. Carlos and Luke headed their way, while Michael went around asking everyone to take their seats. Joe took his place in front of the arbor beside the minister.

Amy's stomach flooded with butterflies. A real wedding. In her backyard. Amanda and Joe's wedding. She pressed a hand to her chest.

The back door opened, and Luke stepped inside. He winked, and her face flushed hot. He leaned in close. "That was quite a wakeup call this morning."

His words sent a thrill down her spine, but she shook her head and backed away. No way were they discussing this now. Or ever, if he'd let her get away with it.

Dorothy handed out bouquets to all the bridesmaids. Outside, music began to play.

"Oh my God," Amanda whispered and pressed a hand to her stomach.

"Okay?" Amy asked.

Amanda nodded. Tears shone in her eyes. "I just can't believe it's finally happening."

The photographer clicked away, documenting the moment.

"Here we go," Dorothy announced cheerfully. She gave her daughter a quick hug, then took Joe's father's arm and headed out the back door.

"We're up next," Luke said and took Becca's arm.

Last week, Amy had been relieved not to be paired up with Luke, but right now, she really wished she were the one on his arm. Becca was holding onto him a little too firmly for Amy's taste, batting her eyelashes and chattering a mile a minute as they walked out the door.

As Luke and Becca started down the aisle, Amy took Michael's arm. She glanced over her shoulder one last time at Amanda. "Love you," she mouthed.

"Love you too," Amanda whispered back, a radiant smile on her face.

Amy stepped out into the bright sunshine with Michael at her side, a sea of faces smiling at them as they walked down the aisle toward the arbor in front. Today, it was draped with lush pink and white flowers.

Luke stood to Joe's right. His eyes met Amy's and held.

"We'd be married with a couple of kids by now," he'd told her twice now.

As she walked toward him, carrying a bouquet, she had to give her head a quick shake to keep out the visions of herself dressed in white. Because her dress today was blue, and they were here to celebrate their friends' wedding. And while she and Luke definitely had some residual chemistry, he was going back to Baltimore after the wedding, and Amy would get back to focusing on Noah. He came first. Always.

She passed Luke to take her place next to Becca. Tara and Carlos came next, and then the music shifted. Everyone's eyes locked on Amanda and her father as they came out of the house.

Tears welled in Amy's eyes. She'd never seen her friend happier than she looked at that moment. And as she stole a peek at Joe, she saw the same joy stamped on his face, along with the awestruck look of a man who's just had his breath taken away by the woman he loves in her wedding gown.

The ceremony went off without a hitch, with Amy and pretty much everyone else sniffling their way through as Amanda and Joe professed their love for each other and were pronounced husband and wife. About a million pictures later, they finally made their way to the tent for refreshments and dancing.

"You look stunning," Luke whispered in her ear.

She glanced up, lost in his endless hazel eyes. Lost because she couldn't imagine him not being here, not being with her after the wedding was over. Maybe a little part of her had been in love with him ever since high school. "Thank you."

"Please tell me you're not drinking Amanda's wine again tonight."

She grimaced. "I'm not drinking *any* wine tonight."

His head dipped closer to hers. "That's good, because I think we have some unfinished business to take care of later."

A warm shiver ran through her. "Do we?"

"I know I do." With a wink and a look that left her breathless, he walked off toward the bar.

"You and Luke have looked awfully intense together this week," Amanda said from behind her.

Amy turned, feeling her cheeks grow hot. "What?"

"Are you two back together?"

"No. I mean, not really, or... I don't know." She pressed a hand to her forehead.

Amanda laughed. "Mm hmm, I know that look. Maybe you want to keep the wedding arbor up in your backyard a little longer?"

"What? No...no way." Amy was stuttering, and she couldn't help it. "I don't think I'll ever get married."

Amanda winked. "Never say never."

* * *

"May I have this dance?" Luke held his hand out.

Amy took it with a smile. The party was well underway now. With Joe's iPhone hooked up to a speaker system in the tent, they had their own readymade DJ. Couples had spilled out onto the lawn to dance in the grass.

And when a slow song started, Luke couldn't resist the chance to hold Amy in his arms. She was absolutely breathtaking tonight in that blue dress that accentuated all her curves. If luck was on his side, he was going to get to take it off her later tonight.

He was damn near dying to find out what she was wearing underneath it, to take that off her too, to make love to her because he had a feeling it would be even better between them now than it had been in high school.

She followed him to the area of the lawn where other couples were dancing and settled in his arms. The sun had dipped below the treetops, setting the evening around them ablaze in pinks and purples. Someone flicked a switch, and strings of white lights lit all around the tent.

"It's beautiful," she whispered.

"It's pretty, but not anywhere near as beautiful as you." He tightened his arms around her, drawing her closer.

"Luke—" Her brow bunched.

"No worrying. Tonight we just see what happens, and tomorrow we'll figure out the rest of it."

She nodded, resting her head against his shoulder. They swayed together to the music, and when Joe's iPhone segued into another slow song, they kept dancing. Amy smelled like some kind of flowery perfume tonight. It was intoxicating. *She* was intoxicating.

"Um." She giggled, glancing down at the front of his pants.

Yeah. He wanted her. Bad. And there was no hiding it. He leaned in to whisper in her ear. "As I recall, this morning's chat was a whole lot more satisfying for you than it was for me."

She looked up at him with wide eyes. "Oh. You mean, you didn't...?"

He shook his head. No, he hadn't wanted anything to distract him from her pleasure. Even if it meant he'd had to take a long, cold shower afterward.

"Oh," she said again, bringing her hips against his.

He groaned. "If you want to know the truth, I just got back in the states a few weeks ago. I was overseas with Doctors Without Borders for eighteen months."

"And you didn't date while you were over there?"

"No. So it's been a *long* time for me."

"Me too," she whispered. "I don't date much—or at all, really. Noah is my priority."

Interesting. "How long?"

"Longer than you."

He chuckled. "So we're both up for some kind of award for celibacy then."

She looked up, her brown eyes hazy with lust. "I'm ready to end that tonight."

Oh, *hallelujah.* Her hips were still flush with his, and his poor aching cock was about to burst through the front of his pants. "Right now, it's really inconvenient that we're not at some hotel where we can just go upstairs to your room and put an end to our reign of celibacy."

"We can't even leave early since it's my house. We're stuck here until every last person goes home." She looked around them at the yard still filled with happy guests.

The universe had a really sick sense of humor sometimes. "Then we keep dancing."

So they did. They danced and danced, but no one seemed to be in any hurry to break up the party. "So tell me," he whispered.

"Yeah?"

"What will we do first?" The night around them was full dark now, lit only by the twinkling white lights around the tent. Here on the lawn only a few other couples remained dancing.

She glanced around them, then smiled. "Well, I'd like to say first we make out for a while, but I'm not sure I'll be able to wait that long."

"As long as I have you, I can wait as long as you need." Which was true, but it was going to take every ounce of his willpower.

"I think we've already waited long enough." Her breath warmed his neck, and he felt his control slipping.

"There's something I've got to know," he said.

"What?"

"What are you wearing under that dress?"

"Well, there's a strapless bra." She paused. "It's lacy, with blue trim. You might like it. And, um, a thong. Also blue and lacy."

"Damn, woman."

She gave him a shy smile. "I was kind of hoping this might happen when I got dressed this morning."

"What, that we'd be stuck on the dance floor for hours waiting for everyone to leave?"

"No," she whispered. "That you'd, you know, stay. Tonight."

Stay. He liked that word. "I was kind of hoping that too."

"A few people have left," she said.

So they had. But the bride and groom were still here, which meant the party was still going. "So, back to tonight. After I take you out of your lacy bra and thong. Then what?"

"What would you like?"

"I'd like to put my mouth on you until you're screaming my name."

Amy let out a little whimper.

Yeah, this was torture, but he couldn't seem to stop. "And then I want to bury myself inside you so deep I—"

"Hey, man!" Joe said loudly beside him.

Luke almost bit his tongue. Amy whirled backward out of his arms. He shoved his hands into his pants pockets to hide himself from embarrassment.

"Am I interrupting something?" Joe asked, glancing between them with an amused look.

"Not at all. We were just talking," Luke said. Dirty talking, but talking.

"Mm hmm. Well, I just wanted to let you know Amanda and I are heading out. She's exhausted, and we leave for Hawaii early tomorrow morning. The guys said they'll come over tomorrow to help clean up everything if that's okay."

"Perfect," Amy said, a little too cheerfully.

"Okay, well good-bye then. And thanks again for everything, Amy."

"It was my pleasure," she said. "Truly."

Luke watched him walk away, then turned to Amy. They stared at each other for a moment, then her lips turned in a wicked smile. "Finally."

Seven

It was another half hour before the last guest left. And then Amanda's parents insisted on hanging around and helping Amy straighten up. She let Yoda run around the yard while they worked. As soon as the last car pulled out of the driveway, she dragged Luke in through the back door of her house. Inside, they stood facing each other for a moment in the near darkness.

"About damn time," he said, then he crushed her against him for a kiss that completely wiped her mind of any rational thought other than getting him into her bed.

"Hurry."

"Baby, I didn't wait fifteen years for another chance with you to hurry once I finally have you all to myself."

A shiver of anticipation rippled through her. She reached down and gripped him through the front of his pants. Oh yeah, he was hard. And was it possible that he was even bigger than she remembered?

Had he really waited fifteen years for another chance with her? That didn't make sense when he'd moved on so quickly after they broke up. He'd married impulsively, then gotten divorced a few years later. Those were the actions of a fickle man, not the man she'd thought she'd known for a few tender years in high school.

Luke swept her off her feet and carried her down the hall to her bedroom, kicking the door shut behind them to keep the dog out. "Now, I think the first thing we talked about was making out for a while."

"Skip it." She pushed his suit jacket over his shoulders.

He set her on the edge of the bed, then shrugged out of the jacket. "No rushing. I mean it." He kissed her, slow and sensual, burning her up from the inside out. Their tongues tangled, and their hands roamed. She pressed her body against his, clinging to him while he kissed her senseless.

And God, the man could kiss. But all that time on the dance floor had taken a toll on her self-control. She brought her hips against his, pressing his erection between her legs, but it wasn't enough. She rocked against him with a whimper of frustration, drawing a low groan from Luke.

"I think the next thing we talked about was getting you out of this dress," he said, his voice strained.

"Hurry." She leaned forward, spreading kisses across his neck while he fumbled with the zipper on her dress.

He tugged at the back of her dress. "Dammit."

"You have to undo the clasp first, then the zipper."

He pulled back for a moment to kiss her. "Why do women's clothes have to be so complicated?"

"Are your hands shaking?" She gripped them in hers.

He looked into her eyes. His were hot and heavy with lust, but it was more than that. He was tender despite his urgency, like he wanted much more than sex. "That's the effect you have on me."

"That, or you've been celibate for too long." She winked, trying to restore the playful mood between them, because right now he looked so serious it was making her heart turn all kinds of crazy cartwheels in her chest.

"This is more than sex. You know that, right?" He kissed the palm of her hand and pressed it against his cheek. "I want you, Amy. All of you, not just your body."

Ah, crap. Now he was talking about emotions, and she didn't know what to say, but then he freed the clasp on the back of her dress and eased down the zipper. His hands were on her bare skin, and she forgot how to speak, forgot everything but the way it felt when he touched her.

No one else had ever seduced her the way Luke could.

He slid the dress over her shoulders, revealing her bra. A low groan tore from his throat as he leaned back, just taking her in. Her skin flushed warm, and she felt the inexplicable urge to touch herself beneath his heated gaze.

"So beautiful," he whispered. He knelt between her knees, trailing kisses down her neck and across her chest. He nipped at the lacy edge of her bra, teasing, tempting, until she arched her back, pressing closer.

He popped the clasp of her bra, and it tumbled to the floor. Then he drew her nipple into his mouth, teasing with his tongue until the ache between her legs grew almost too strong to bear. She shifted restlessly, fisting her hands in his hair to hold him close.

His hand trailed down her belly, dipping inside the dress where it had pooled around her waist. His fingers traced the edge of her panties, and a needy whimper escaped her throat. It had been so long, so very long, since a man had touched her. "Please," she whispered.

"Oh, baby, I'm just getting started." He dipped his hand between her legs, touching her through her panties, and her body went up in flames. She was already so close, and he'd barely touched her. "But first I need to finish undressing you."

He tugged her forward into his arms, and the dress slid to the floor. He looked down, and his eyes darkened. "Damn, baby, you are so gorgeous."

She didn't believe that for a minute, except...beneath his gaze she *did* feel gorgeous. He was looking at her like she was the most beautiful woman he'd ever seen. She reached down and tugged at her panties. They hit the floor, and Luke sucked in a breath.

"I think the next thing I said was that I'd put my mouth on you until you screamed my name." His voice had gone low and husky, and *oh God,* so sexy.

"But you're still dressed..."

He pushed her back on the bed. "I can wait." He kissed the inside of her thigh, and she gasped. His mouth was hot, the sensation almost too much to handle. He kissed his way up her leg until he reached the apex of her thighs. There he paused. Then he kissed her, and she let out an embarrassingly needy squeak.

She whimpered and squirmed as he drove her wild with his mouth. Stars were already dancing behind her eyelids, and before she knew it, an orgasm exploded through her, rocking her to her core. "Luke!" Her voice was a hoarse whisper.

He coaxed her higher with his tongue, taking her right outside herself with pleasure, and *holy shit.* She wasn't sure she'd ever felt anything so amazing.

"Damn, that was hot." Luke flopped onto the bed next to her, his eyes glittering in the near darkness. "I forgot how sexy you are when you come."

"And I don't remember you being this much of a dirty talker," she whispered, still breathless from the orgasm he'd just given her.

"I've grown up. So have you."

"I like the grown-up version." And yeah, she was talking about more than just his body too. "But you're wearing too many clothes."

He laughed roughly. "Sure am."

She slid forward to straddle his lap, unbuttoning her way down the front of his shirt, but he was still hard, *so hard,* and it was highly distracting. Luke let out a strangled sound, his hands gripping her butt, pressing her more firmly against him. She rocked her hips, thrilled at the way her body responded to his, already wanting more, already aching for the kind of release only he could give her.

"Amy—" His voice was strained as he thrust himself against her. "I have never wanted anyone as much as I want you right now."

"That's probably the celibacy talking," she joked.

"That certainly isn't helping, but it's you, Amy." He crushed her against him with another heady kiss. "It's always been you. Only you."

Their bodies were entwined now, kissing, touching, *desperate.* She fumbled the last buttons of his shirt, and he tossed it to the floor. Then she reached for his pants. He groaned as she undid the button, her fingers brushing against him. She slid her hand down his length as she lowered his zipper, and he thrust against her palm.

He scrambled out of his pants and boxer briefs, and then he was finally, gloriously naked. His body was lean but muscular in a way he hadn't been back in high school. He was a man now, not a teenager. A man who trembled beneath her touch as she traced her fingers down his chest and took him in her hand. He was so very big, so hard. For her.

"Now, Luke. I can't wait another minute."

He let out what might have been a laugh or a groan and dove for the side of the bed. He came up with a condom, tore open the package, and rolled it on in record time.

"Only you, Amy," he whispered as he positioned himself over her. And with one long stroke, he slid inside.

They clung to each other, desperate and overcome. He thrust once, long and slow, then picked up the pace, matching the thrust of her hips with his. He felt so good, *so good*, inside her. As good—better—than it had ever been.

She burned for him, the ache inside her rising, growing, building until she thought she might burst from it. "Luke," she whimpered, pressing him even deeper inside her.

"Amy..." He swiveled his hips, thrusting faster, and she broke.

She screamed his name as pleasure exploded inside her, hotter and brighter than anything she'd ever felt before. Luke groaned, thrusting faster, harder. His body tensed as he found his own release.

They lay like that for a long time, not moving, their bodies still joined.

"Only you," he whispered again, and her heart swelled inside her chest.

Only Luke. There had never been anyone else. But after everything that had happened between them, how could she ever really trust him with her heart?

* * *

If there had been any doubt in Luke's mind before, now he knew: he was in love with Amy Jameson. Maybe he'd always loved her. And he had this one night to show her how he felt and how much she still meant to him. He had to give her a night she'd never forget.

"Do you want cake?" she whispered beside him.

"Cake sounds great."

She slipped out of bed, went to the dresser against the wall, and pulled out some kind of pink shirt-dress, which she tugged over her head. He stood and pulled his boxer briefs and pants back on, then followed her down the hall to the living room.

Yoda trotted at their heels.

"Be right back." He gave her a quick kiss and walked outside to his SUV. Since he'd been hoping like hell the night would end like this, he'd packed a duffel bag because he did not want to wear this suit home tomorrow.

He grabbed the bag and went inside. Amy was in the kitchen, presumably stealing a couple of slices of wedding cake for them, so he went down the hall and changed into khaki shorts. He tucked a condom in the back pocket, just in case. When he made it back to the living room, she was waiting with a big slice of leftover wedding cake on a plate.

His stomach rumbled.

"I didn't have a chance to eat any earlier," she said. "I was a bit distracted."

He sat and pulled her into his lap. "Same."

She'd brought two forks and handed him one. "Tell me more about your work with Doctors Without Borders. What was it like? What countries did you visit?"

He forked a chunk of cake into his mouth, chewed, and swallowed. "I spent almost a year in Iraq, primarily working with Syrian refugees. I delivered babies and treated injuries. There are so many innocent people over there who have nothing to do with the war but have no access to medical care because of it."

Amy turned her head to meet his gaze. "I had no idea. Were you in danger?"

He shrugged. "Some. But I needed to be there. I had been feeling so...restless here at home. I don't know how to explain it, but I needed to spend some time doing something for someone else for a change."

She kissed him. "I get that, but I'm so glad you made it home safely."

He turned her in his lap so that she faced him. "Things in Baltimore weren't satisfying me anymore. I did my thing overseas, and it was great, but that's not it either. I need more, Amy. I'm ready to settle down. I want a family. I want *you.*"

She drew back. "You said tonight was just about having fun, and we'd worry about the rest tomorrow."

He pressed a gentle kiss to her lips. "You're right; I did. I'm sorry."

They were quiet as they demolished the rest of the slice of cake. She wiggled her butt against him and gave him a look. "Again?"

How could he not get aroused with her sitting in his lap? "We have a lot of lost time to make up for."

"Yes, we do." She stood and tugged him toward the back door.

"Where are we going?"

"A replay of earlier tonight," she said with a giggle.

He wasn't sure what that meant, but he followed her anyway. Her backyard still looked like a wedding venue. The chairs and arbor were still there, the tent and tables still in place. Amy bent down behind the tent, and the twinkling white lights came back on. She led him over to the grassy area of the lawn where they'd danced for so long earlier, waiting for everyone to leave.

"But this time, no one's here," she whispered.

"Just us." He pulled her into his arms, and they swayed together to the song of the crickets and cicadas buzzing in the trees around them.

"No neighbors," she said, pressing her hips against his.

"Which means this time I can touch you." He reached under her skirt and palmed her ass.

"And I can touch you." She ran her hand down the front of his shorts, and his cock surged beneath her touch.

"I get the better end of this deal," he said, sliding his hand between her legs.

She gasped as he touched her bare skin. "I wouldn't be so sure about that." She slid her hand inside his shorts and gripped him.

"This is the kinkiest wedding I've ever been to." He stroked her, rewarded by her needy gasps and the way her hips thrust against his hand.

"Mm hmm." She stroked up and down his shaft, and damn if he didn't need her every bit as badly as he had earlier tonight. His cock ached beneath her touch, and when she swirled her fingers over his head, he damn near came in his shorts.

He tipped his head to hers and kissed her, drinking her in, his tongue tangling with hers. They swayed together beneath the twinkling lights, touching, teasing, stroking, until Amy pressed her hips against his. "Now."

And he mentally high fived himself for putting that condom in his back pocket earlier. He unzipped his shorts, rolled it on, and lifted her into his arms. Her legs went around his waist, and she lifted her hips so that his cock pressed against her center. And then she sank onto him.

They both gasped. He clutched her in his arms, his cock buried inside her. His body burned. Amy squirmed with a needy whimper. Holding her close, he walked into the house. Each step rocked her slightly against him, and by the time he lowered them onto the couch, he was so far gone he was already seeing stars.

He held her in his lap, and they made love, raw and hot and needy. As he poured himself into her, he knew there was no one else for him.

Only Amy.

But did she feel the same?

Eight

Amy woke to bright sunlight and that feeling of mild panic that every mother feels when she realizes she's overslept. *Where's Noah? Why didn't he wake me?*

But then Luke stirred beside her, and she knew. It was Sunday. Noah was camping with T.J. And she'd slept in because she and Luke had been up late doing all sorts of naughty things. Her body was sore in some mighty interesting places this morning.

"Mornin'," Luke said, his voice low and gravelly from sleep.

"Good morning." She rolled to face him.

God, he looked good first thing in the morning. His face was covered in a delicious amount of stubble, his eyes still soft from sleep. Amy, on the other hand, probably looked a hot mess.

Had she even washed her face before bed last night? She couldn't remember. She reached up self-consciously to smooth her hair.

"You look gorgeous," he said, as if he'd read her mind.

"And you're a liar." She nudged him playfully with her fist.

"I never lie." He grabbed her fist and tugged her in closer.

And, oh yeah, they were both naked. And Luke was already fully aroused.

And now, so was she.

"Plans for the day?" he asked as he nibbled the side of her neck, going straight for the sensitive spot that had always been her undoing.

She snuggled in closer against his body. "More of this?"

"Sounds good to me." His hands wandered down her sides, touching and caressing as they went.

She pulled back to look at him. "Noah will be back this afternoon."

"I figured that."

"So, I think you should go home before then."

His brow furrowed. "Why? I like hanging out with him, and, unless I'm wrong, I think he likes hanging out with me too."

"He does, but there's a big difference between Mr. Luke, the guy who's helping get the house ready for a wedding, and Mr. Luke, the guy who's...whatever we're doing."

"You don't think he'll like us dating?"

"I don't know." She bit her lip and looked away. "I haven't really dated since his dad left us. Change is hard for Noah, any kind of change. He needs things in his life that are permanent, and I'm not sure that this is."

"Seriously?" Luke sat up and looked at her. "What the hell does that mean?"

"It means we slept together last night, and I'd rather keep Noah out of it until we figure out the rest, okay?"

He nodded, but there was a new kind of energy between them as they made love in the soft morning light. Something raw, desperate even. As if everything might blow up in their faces if they dared look too hard at what they were doing.

Reality.

That's what it was. By the time she and Luke sat down at the kitchen table to eat breakfast, reality was slapping her hard in the face. Sure, last night had been wonderful. Magical. Certainly the most romantic night of her life.

But that didn't mean a relationship with Luke was a good idea. They had a rocky history, and he didn't even live in Dogwood anymore. This was exactly why she didn't date. She just didn't have the time—or the energy—to figure this stuff out.

She'd just bitten into her blueberry muffin when the front door burst open and Noah walked in.

T.J. stood behind him, hat in hand, a sheepish look on his face. "Sorry, I tried to stop him when I saw the car in the driveway, but he, uh..." He shook his head. "Anyway, we had a great time camping. I'll check in with you later."

He closed the front door behind him. A moment later, she heard his truck roar to life.

Noah stood in the middle of the living room, still wearing his backpack, his hands fluttering restlessly at his sides. "Why is Mr. Luke here?"

Her son felt uncomfortable in his own home. And that was totally and completely her fault. She lurched from the kitchen table, grabbing at Luke's arm. "Mr. Luke was just leaving. I'll walk him out while you go put your backpack away in your bedroom. Okay, Noah?"

He nodded as he walked down the hall toward his bedroom, Yoda at his side.

Amy tugged at Luke's hand until he stood from the table. "Go get your bag."

He gave her a dark look, then went down the hall to her bedroom, returning with his duffle bag in hand. She practically dragged him out the front door.

"What the hell?" He stared at her, his hazel eyes snapping. "Why are you making this so awkward?"

"It's time for you to go."

"Noah's home early so you're just going to throw me out of the house?"

She crossed her arms over her chest. "Change upsets him. You being here just now was upsetting for him."

"Noah comes first," he said, his tone softening. "I get that, and that's how it should be. But he knows me, Amy. Is it such a big fucking deal for him to see me eat a muffin in your kitchen?"

"Maybe not, but I don't want him to get used to seeing you around, because then when you're not, he'll get hurt."

Luke stepped closer, his eyes boring into hers. "Who says I won't be around?"

"Your track record does. I was miserable after I dumped you in high school. But while I was working up the courage to come after you and beg for another chance, you had already moved on with another girl. A girl who you *married*." She practically spat the word at him. She wasn't being fair. She knew it, but she didn't care.

"Wait a damn minute—"

"I did." Her voice was softer now. "I did wait for you. You promised to love me forever, and then you spent what, a day at college missing me? And you fell in love with Georgia. And you promised to love *her* forever. Or I assume you did because you married her. But then you divorced her. So, no, I don't think you're very likely to stick around long-term."

"You've got it all wrong." And damn him, he looked hurt.

"No, I don't. Those are the facts. And I can't..." She drew a shaky breath. "I just can't have my heart broken again. Especially not by you."

And then she went inside and closed the door behind her.

* * *

Luke had no idea what the hell had just happened. He'd gone from blissfully happy in Amy's bed to thrown out the front door and dumped—again—in a matter of minutes. But one thing he knew for sure: this time he was coming back to set things straight. And another thing: he needed to tell her everything that had happened his first year of college.

Because she was so wrong. He'd always loved Amy.

And this time, he was going to prove it.

He went home to his mom's house, but he was so distracted she called him on it before lunchtime.

"What's going on, Luke?"

"Amy," he just said that one word because his mom knew. She'd always known.

"You spent the night at her place."

"And she dumped me this morning."

She frowned at him. "What did you do?"

"Nothing, Mom. I swear. I was just sitting there eating breakfast when Noah got home, and she freaked out about Noah seeing us together, which turned into a rehash of how I married Georgia five seconds after she dumped me the first time."

"Oh, honey. Well, you've got to go talk to her."

"I will, but not today. I've got to go when Noah's not there."

"And you've got to be romantic," his mom said. "Amy's going to need a big gesture. Something that shows her how much you love her, how much you've *always* loved her."

And Luke thought he might have an idea of how to do just that.

Nine

The week was off to a horrible start. Amy had finally gotten everything cleaned up from the wedding—which was a lot less fun without having Luke around—and her damned AC was out again. She and Noah had suffered through two days of sweltering heat. Two nights where she'd tossed and turned, remembering the things she and Luke had done in this bed.

And in her backyard. And on her couch.

Dammit, the whole house would torment her forever with memories.

She'd left the arbor up in the backyard. It was pretty, and it would look great with a little bench beneath it. She could sit there and work or read with Noah.

Two days, and not a word from Luke.

He was probably engaged to someone new by now. She balled her fists and pressed them against her eyes to keep the tears at bay. She knew she was being overly dramatic. But dammit, why did she keep pushing away the only man she'd ever loved? And why did he keep walking away without a second glance?

She was an idiot. And Luke was a jerk.

End of story.

Noah ran across the backyard, Yoda at his heels. He grabbed the worn tennis ball Merry had sent over with the dog and chucked it across the yard. Yoda sprinted after it, grabbed it, and kept running.

"Not so good at fetching, is he?" she said.

Noah shook his head. "Maybe he doesn't understand the rules. Why doesn't Mr. Luke come over anymore?"

"Well, he was helping get our house ready for the wedding, and now the wedding's over." Amy ignored the pinch in her heart at Luke's name.

"I miss him," Noah said.

She looked down at her hands. "Yeah, me too."

"Then why don't you ask him to come over? I want to show him that Brick Tricks video with the submarine."

If only it were that easy. "He'll probably be going back to Baltimore soon."

"I think he'd be a good stepdad," Noah said, echoing their conversation last week. "You said if you married Mr. Luke, he'd be my stepdad. So you should invite him over." And with that bombshell, he walked off across the backyard.

Shit. She'd pushed Luke away to protect Noah. Had she been wrong? Did it even matter anymore?

She sat in the rocking chair on the patio and watched Noah and Yoda play. Noah tossed the ball, and they ran together after it. The dog always kept an eye on Noah, watching over him, never straying far from his side. They were incredibly in sync that way. With Yoda, Noah ran, and laughed, and played like a happy, carefree nine-year-old. Something he hadn't always been, not before Yoda came to stay with them.

She'd never thought she could have a dog with her allergies, but this little poodle mix didn't cause her any trouble as long as she took her daily allergy meds. His food and care were expensive, but *Everyday Emmy* was still bringing in enough money to cover the difference and then some.

"Noah," she called.

He jogged toward her, a wide smile on his face, Yoda bouncing at his heels.

"Do you think you're ready for the responsibility of having your own dog?"

Noah's eyes grew impossibly wide behind his glasses. "Oh, yes. I would walk him, and feed him, and take care of him. I'd even poop-scoop the yard."

It was true too. He already did all of those things for Yoda, and Amy had no doubt he would continue to help. "I'd need you to keep helping out with all of those things."

"Mom," Noah looked right into her eyes, his expression so joyous her heart rolled over in her chest. "You're talking about Yoda, right? About keeping Yoda?"

"Yeah, bud." She tugged him into her arms for a big hug. "We're going to keep Yoda."

"My dog." Happy tears streaked Noah's cheeks. "Yoda, you're my dog now. I'm going to love you forever."

Amy wiped her eyes as Noah took his dog inside to make him a permanent home in his bedroom. *Permanent.*

She sat with her laptop later that night, blogging about her newest family member, and it struck her: why was she more comfortable sharing these intimate moments with nameless, faceless strangers on the internet than anyone in her real life? She closed her eyes and imagined Luke here with her, helping celebrate Yoda's adoption into the family.

I think he'd be a good stepdad.

Yeah, she did too. And maybe she should go after him. Apologize. But if he really wanted another chance with her, why had he walked away—again—without a fight?

* * *

On Wednesday, Amy spent the morning working at the diner as usual. At least it was air conditioned. The AC repairman was coming later today, and already her stomach was in knots about how much it would cost to fix this time. Almost certainly more than she had to spend.

Her feet were dragging by the time she got home. She didn't want to go inside and face the heat. Or the lonely house full of memories.

But Luke's SUV was parked in her driveway.

Excitement warred with anger inside her. What was he doing here? Even if he'd come to ask for another chance, what could he possibly say that would convince her to trust him after the way he'd acted in the past?

Cautiously, she parked in the driveway and got out of her car. Luke's SUV was empty. Her house was locked, and he didn't have a key, which meant he must be...out back?

She drew a deep breath as she walked around the side of the house. Sure enough, Luke stood beneath the arbor, one foot crossed over the other, looking so ridiculously handsome that her heart missed a beat.

So handsome that it took her several long seconds to notice that the arbor was once again draped in flowers. Instead of the lush pink and white peonies and roses that had adorned it during the wedding, today it had been decorated more boldly with bright reds, oranges, and purples. The flowers had been stuck haphazardly through its framework. In fact, it almost looked like a man—perhaps a certain sexy doctor—had decorated it himself.

"I have a story to tell you," Luke said.

"Um. Okay." She stopped halfway across the yard, keeping some space between them. What kind of story did he want to tell her?

"There once was a teenage boy named Luke, and he loved Amy with all his heart. He thought he might even be lucky enough to spend the rest of his life with her."

She was silent. Where was he going with this? She already knew this story.

"But she was afraid he might be a jerk and break her heart once he went off to college without her, so she broke up with him. And Luke, well, he had no idea what to do without her. He was heartbroken, but he was also young and stupid, so he slept with a pretty girl from his anatomy class named Georgia, thinking it might help him get over Amy."

"Luke," she interrupted him. "I really don't need to hear this."

"But you do," he said quietly, "because Georgia got pregnant."

She sucked in a breath. "But...there was no baby." And now she felt sick to her stomach.

"No." He shoved his hands into his pockets. "But I tried to do the right thing, Amy, by asking her to marry me. When she lost the baby, we were both devastated. It brought us together, but we were never in love, not really. Not the way I loved you, the way I still love you." He looked into her eyes so that she could see the truth reflected there. "But what kind of jerk would I be if I broke off our engagement because she lost our baby?"

The worst kind. And Luke wasn't a jerk. In her heart, she knew that.

"I'm sorry," she whispered.

"Georgia and I got married for all the wrong reasons, for a baby that was never born, and so it didn't work out. We probably had the friendliest breakup in history, because neither of us were heartbroken; we were never really in love."

As he spoke, she walked toward him across the lawn until she was standing right in front of him, the arbor overhead and Luke's hazel eyes staring straight into hers. The power of his gaze was so intense she thought he must be looking all the way into her soul.

He took her hands in his. "My mistake, the only one I can apologize for, is in walking away from you without a fight back then. You are the most amazing woman in the world, and I should have moved heaven and earth to win you back. But I was a stupid, horny teenager, and I did a stupid thing and slept with a girl I hardly knew. Can you forgive me?"

She nodded as tears welled in her eyes. "As long as you didn't do the same stupid thing when I dumped you last weekend."

He shook his head with a laugh. "Amy, I promise you, I never want to be with anyone but you ever again." He brought her hands to his lips and kissed her knuckles. "You're the only woman I've ever loved. I think I've been in love with you my whole life."

Oh, her heart! She tried to press a hand to her chest, but Luke was still holding her hands, and now his hands were on her chest, his palm against her heart, and it was thumping like a bongo drum. "I love you too. Always you. Only you."

And then she was in his arms, and he was kissing her like his life depended on it, and nothing had ever felt so right. Her arms were around his neck, her body pressed to his, breathing him in, wanting to absorb absolutely everything about this moment.

He raised his head and looked at her. "I know you're worried about what would happen to Noah if I leave, but I promise you, I never will. In fact, I have a very important question to ask you."

She swallowed hard. "Okay."

He reached into his pocket and pulled out a little blue box at the same time he dropped down to one knee in front of the brightly decorated arbor.

"Oh my God." She pressed a hand to her mouth.

"Amy Jameson, will you make me the happiest man on earth and say you'll be my wife?" He opened the blue box and held it toward her, revealing the ring inside. It was absolutely the most gorgeous thing she'd ever seen, with a diamond glittering in the middle, surrounded by tiny bead-cut stones.

"Yes. Oh my God, yes."

He took her left hand and slid the ring into place, his fingers leaving behind a trail of warmth. For a moment, they both stared at the ring on her finger.

"Wow," she said finally.

"Yeah." He stood and tugged her into his arms. "About damn time you have my ring on your finger. I love you so much, Amy. I never want to spend another minute without you."

"And Noah?"

"Of course, Noah." He grinned. "I love him too. You know that, right?"

She nodded, blinking back tears. She did know it. She'd seen it every time he and Noah had been together these last few weeks. And now, with Luke, her son would finally have a true father figure in his life.

"I'm sorry it took me so long to come here," he said. "I knew you needed more than an apology. I wanted to do this right, and it took me a couple of days to put it all together."

"Worth the wait," she whispered, kissing him again. *So* worth the wait. She'd remember this moment for the rest of her life.

They stood together under the arbor, kissing and talking, until she heard the squealing brakes of the school bus out front.

"Let's go tell him," she said, taking Luke's hand.

"I can't wait."

Neither could she.

Epilogue

Amy's backyard was once again the scene of a wedding. Today, the arbor dripped with red roses, yellow sunflowers, and gerbera daisies in every color. The trees behind it reflected the changing season with red and yellow leaves.

The perfect setting for a fall wedding.

Amy drew a deep breath and pressed a hand against the front of her ivory dress.

Beside her, Amanda giggled. "Full circle since this spring, huh?" She rubbed a hand over her belly, round now with her and Joe's baby due in just a few weeks.

"In more ways than one," Amy said.

Noah, looking impossibly handsome in his little gray tux, nodded solemnly. "My mom has a baby in her belly too."

Merry leaped off the couch, nearly tossing her bouquet in the process. "Shut the front door! Are you serious?"

"I'm always serious," Noah told her.

Merry doubled over in laughter. "That's true, buddy, you are. And I love that about you." She tousled his brown hair. "Congratulations, Amy. That's fantastic news."

"I have to say," Amy said, eyeing her new sister-in-law, "I thought you and T.J. would beat us to it."

Merry's face turned a funny shade of red. "Actually..."

"No way." Amy felt happy tears well in her eyes. "You too?"

Merry nodded. "Eight weeks."

Amanda laughed. "This has got to be the most fertile wedding party ever."

"What does that mean?" Noah asked.

"Well, it means there are going to be a lot of babies around here soon," Merry told him.

He bent down to pet Yoda. "Oh. Is it time to walk down the aisle yet?"

"Just about. Here come Grandma and Grandpa now." Amy looked out the back window to see her parents headed their way. Butterflies swarmed her stomach. She'd never thought this day would happen. *Her wedding day.*

And yet here she was, marrying Luke. Her first love. The only man who'd ever truly owned her heart. Happiness swelled warm and bright inside her.

Since their reunion that spring, Luke had taken a job at Dogwood Hospital and moved in with her and Noah, and their little house had never felt more like home. With *Everyday Emmy* continuing to grow in popularity, Amy was considering quitting her job at the diner when the baby was born, a luxury she never would have considered even a few short months ago.

Her parents came through the back door. EmmyLou was radiant in a blue dress. Trace looked handsome and distinguished in a gray tuxedo similar to Noah's. Her father had accented his with a bolo tie and cowboy boots.

"Oh, sweetie, I'm so happy I could just burst." Her mother pulled her in for a hug.

"Me too, Mom."

"First T.J., and now it's your turn. Both of my babies married, and I'm getting the best son and daughter-in-law out of the deal too." EmmyLou smiled warmly at Merry.

The music outside changed. EmmyLou gave Amy a big hug then turned to Noah. "What do you say, are you ready to walk me down the aisle?"

He nodded and followed her out the back door, Yoda trotting at his side.

Amy choked back tears watching her son walk her mother down the aisle. Merry and T.J. went next, followed by Amanda and Joe.

Amy's dad put his elbow out for her to take his arm. "This is an awfully proud moment for me, Amy. I couldn't be happier for you and Luke."

"Thanks, Dad."

They stepped through the doorway into the bright sunlight outside. Everything felt like slow-motion as they walked, so many happy faces smiling her way. But one face in particular held her attention. Her eyes locked on Luke standing beneath the arbor.

He wore a gray tux and a smile that made her chest swell with happiness. So handsome. And he was hers. By the time she reached him, tears were streaming down her face.

Luke's eyes were glossy too.

The ceremony passed in a blur. Amy felt the breeze in her hair, smelled the sweet aroma of the flowers overhead. She recited her vows, her gaze never wavering from Luke's. Noah brought their rings, looking so grown up it made her heart ache for the awesome little man he was becoming.

"With this ring, I thee wed," Luke said as he slid the platinum band onto her finger.

"With this ring, I thee wed." Her voice wobbled, and she almost dropped the ring.

"I now pronounce you husband and wife," the minister said.

Luke dipped his head toward hers. "You take my breath away, Mrs. Benson. I am the luckiest man alive to call myself your husband."

And then he kissed her, and everything else faded away. There was only Luke. And a lifetime of happiness ahead.

Excerpt from UNLEASHED

Love to the Rescue Book 1

Link to list of buy links: http://www.rachellacey.com/unleashed/

Chapter 1

Cara Medlen felt the growl before she heard it, rumbling against her leg from the dog tensed at her side. She jiggled the leash to break his concentration. "Easy, Casper. You may not realize it yet, but today's your lucky day."

He looked up at her with dull eyes, one brown, one blue. A jagged scar creased his face. Ribs and hip bones jutted through his mangy white coat. And, oh boy, did he stink. Cara had yet to meet an ugly boxer, but Casper...well, he had the sort of face that made people cross to the other side of the street.

That same face grabbed at a tender spot in her heart.

" It's a blessing that Triangle Boxer Rescue can take him," the woman behind the desk, a volunteer named Helen, said. "Shelter life hasn't been good for him."

Cara nodded as she handed the signed paperwork to Helen. "I've worked with a lot of dogs like Casper. I'm sure we'll have him ready for adoption in no time."

But the warning she'd received from her homeowners' association over the summer weighed heavily on her mind: Keep her foster dogs in line or face disciplinary action by the board.

The door to the kennels opened, allowing raucous barking to spill into the lobby. Casper peered around her and fixed his gaze on the man who'd come through the door. His ears flattened, and the hair raised along his spine.

Yep, this dog was trouble all right.

Cara sidestepped to block his view. "Thanks, Helen. Happy New Year."

With a quick wave, she hustled Casper out the front door. He tucked his tail against the cold air, then raised his nose and sniffed the sweet scent of freedom. He slunk onto the brown patchy grass of the shelter's front lawn and raised his leg on a tree.

When he'd finished, she loaded him into the backseat of her little blue Mazda. She smoothed her hands over her black dress, wrinkled since the funeral by hours in the car and now covered in Casper's white fur. The ache in her chest rose up, squeezing her throat, and she shoved it back.

Later, she'd grieve. Now she needed to get Casper home.

She swung into the front seat and cranked the engine. "So, you've officially been sprung from doggy jail."

He gave her a wary look, then turned his head to stare out the window. She pulled onto High Street and took the ramp to Interstate 85, headed for her townhouse in Dogwood, a small town on the outskirts of Raleigh, North Carolina.

"But listen, no more shenanigans, okay?"

Casper cocked his head, his mismatched eyes somber.

"One of my fosters growled at my neighbor's dog, and she filed a complaint against me with the homeowners' association, so I need you to be on your best behavior."

With a dramatic sigh, he sprawled across the backseat and closed his eyes. Well, she'd take that as a yes. She'd put in a few extra hours of behavior training with him in the meantime, just to be sure. Casper slept for the next hour as Cara drove them home.

The latest Taylor Swift single strummed happily from inside her purse, and she shoved a hand inside to grab her cell phone. Merry Atwater's name showed on the display. "Hey, Merry."

"Hey. Just wanted to see how you're holding up," Merry said. "I've been thinking about you all day."

Cara tightened her grip on the steering wheel, blinking away the image of Gina's pale face inside the casket. "I'm okay, or I will be."

"Oh, sweetie, I'm so sorry. Let me know if there's anything I can do. Are you still planning to go out tonight?"

"Yeah, I'll be there, just maybe late. Casper and I have some acquainting to do."

"How is he?" Merry shifted into her professional voice. As the founder of Triangle Boxer Rescue, she had a vested interest in every dog they saved. Cara had no idea where she found the time to run a rescue on top of her day job as a pediatric nurse, but Merry somehow managed to juggle the two.

"Well, he's only growled twice so far." Cara glanced over her shoulder with a smile. Casper watched, his head on his front paws.

"What happened? The shelter didn't mention aggression."

Cara flipped on her blinker and exited the highway onto Fullers Church Road. "I think he's just stressed out. I'm not too worried about it. What time should I meet you at Red Heels?"

"Why don't I come over to your place and we can get ready together? I'll help you get Casper settled, and we can talk."

"Sounds great, Mer, thanks."

"You bet. See you around seven."

Cara shoved the phone back into her purse. Truthfully, the last thing she wanted to do tonight was go to a New Year's Eve party, but she refused to sit home and feel sorry for herself. She'd go, and she'd even have fun, dammit.

It was what Gina would have wanted.

She pulled into the parking lot of Crestwood Gardens, her townhouse community, and guided her Mazda into its assigned spot, right next to her sexy next-door neighbor's shiny black Jeep Grand Cherokee. The man in question stood in his front yard, deep in conversation with a perky brunette in tight jeans and a low-cut sweater.

Cara felt a twinge of something like jealousy, which was ridiculous because she didn't even know his name. And she'd prefer to keep it that way. She shut off the engine and hurried to fetch Casper from the backseat. "Welcome home, dude."

He hopped down, tail tucked. It had been a long and difficult day for both of them. Time to get settled in and relax for a while.

One of her neighbors—Chuck Something-or-other—passed with a nod as Cara headed toward her townhouse. She offered a polite smile, her attention focused on Casper. The dog looked up at the older man. Their eyes met. The hair along Casper's spine raised, and he released a low, guttural growl that sent Chuck scrambling into the parking lot.

Cara swore under her breath as she shoved the key into the lock and pushed open her front door.

So much for making a good first impression on the neighbors.

* * *

Matt Dumont scrubbed a hand over his jaw as his Realtor snapped one last photo of the front of his townhouse. He watched peripherally as his elusive next-door neighbor scrambled through her front door with the mangy, miserable-looking dog who'd just growled at Chuck Sawyer.

It was a different damn dog than he'd seen in her yard last week.

In fact, from what he'd seen, there was a veritable parade of dogs in and out of her home, many of them looking rough, although this one had to be the worst. Matt didn't have much of an eye for dog breeds, but it looked like a pit bull from where he was standing.

He was starting to think something shady was going on next door.

"The listing will be live later tonight. It shows well, so I'm hopeful it will sell relatively quickly." Stephanie Powell pocketed her camera and pulled a red-and-white For Sale sign from her trunk.

He shifted his attention to the business at hand. "Mind if I do the honors?"

"Go ahead." She held it out.

Matt gripped the sign. With a grunt, he shoved the sign-post through the grass and into the hard, red clay beneath. At least here in North Carolina the ground was still pliable at the end of December. Boston's frigid winters would be a re-adjustment.

But he could snowboard again. Yeah, he missed snowboarding, and skiing, and his mom's homemade meatballs. He was ready to go home.

He nudged the sign, then wiggled it a little farther into the earth. Satisfied it wasn't going anywhere, he turned to Stephanie. "All set, then."

She nodded. "I'll be in touch, and hopefully we'll have some showings scheduled for you in the next week."

"Great, Stephanie. Thanks." He shook her hand and headed for the front door of his townhouse, his thoughts again turning to the girl next door and her odd collection of dogs.

Matt knew most of his neighbors, was friendly with all of them, yet she remained a mystery. He didn't even know her name. Perhaps that was why her face sometimes occupied his mind as he passed the long nights on surveillance.

His cell phone rang, and he swiped it from his back pocket. Felicity Prentiss. Shit.

"Mrs. Prentiss," he said as he strode toward his front door.

"I'm having second thoughts." Her voice was taut with nervous energy.

Matt held in a groan. He'd known when he met her yesterday that she was going to be a pain in the ass. Probably, he should have turned her down, but this job would bring in a lot of billable hours, extra cash to tide him over while he got things going up in Boston.

But honestly, Felicity Prentiss was one of the most uptight clients he'd ever worked with. Since she'd hired him yesterday, she'd already called five times, looking for updates, reassurances, and advice.

The woman needed someone to hold her hand. And that was not his job.

Not her husband's, either, since she had enlisted Matt's investigative services to secure evidence of his adultery for their divorce proceedings.

"I'll be honest with you, Mrs. Prentiss. I've never worked one of these cases where it turned out the spouse wasn't cheating. You want proof, I'll get it for you. You want to call it off, tell me now before there's no going back."

On the other end of the line, she sucked in a shaky breath. "I do want to know—I need to know. But what if he sees you? He'd kill me if he knew I'd had him followed."

Matt closed and locked the front door behind him. "He won't see me. Is your husband violent, Mrs. Prentiss?"

"No." A long pause, then a sigh. "No, he's a sweet and gentle man, or at least I thought he was until I caught him sneaking into the house in the middle of the night smelling of another woman's perfume."

"All right, then. Let me do my job. I'll get what you need for the lawsuit, and your husband will be none the wiser. Don't worry."

"It's just...with the New Year and all, I'm ready to get on with my life, you know?"

Did he ever. Matt flipped on the overhead light and sank into his leather recliner. "I do, and you will. Since you'll be with him tonight, I plan to start surveillance tomorrow. Shouldn't take more than a week, maybe two."

Felicity Prentiss hoped to file an "alienation of affection" lawsuit, taking advantage of an outdated law in North Carolina that allowed a wife to sue her husband's lover. The problem was that Felicity couldn't file for divorce from her philandering husband until the necessary evidence had been gathered.

Matt planned to get the evidence she needed for her lawsuit and her divorce proceedings as quickly as possible. Because once he closed this case, he was going home.

He headed upstairs to log some background information on the Prentisses in his office. It always paid to know whose closets you were poking around in before you brought out the high-powered lens. A loud bark drew him toward the window in the hall, from which he had a decent view of his next-door neighbor's backyard.

Enough to see her outside with the white dog and another larger brown dog. She'd changed from her black dress and pumps into an ice-blue jacket and dark-colored jeans that hugged a shapely figure. Her hair was the color of his fantasies, somewhere between blond and red, a delicious apricot that shone in the sun with soft waves that brushed her shoulders.

As he watched, the white dog snarled. The brown dog hesitated a moment, then they were on each other like a couple of wild animals, growling and snapping. The sound made the hair on the back of his neck rise.

Blood streaked the white dog's fur.

Holy shit. Was his pretty golden-haired neighbor training fighting dogs?

With a grunt of disgust, Matt stepped away from the window. It was time for them to finally meet, because there was no way in hell he was going to look the other way if she was mistreating those dogs.

* * *

The dogs were fighting.

"Hey!" Cara clapped her hands and shouted, making as much noise as she could. Casper slunk off to hide behind a bush. Mojo trotted over, looking sheepish.

Cara knelt and ran her hands over him, checking for injury. She suspected the skirmish had been more bark than bite, but with Mojo's dark fur, it was hard to be sure, and she'd seen blood on Casper.

Mojo sat, tongue lolling, tail wagging, as she checked him out. Blood oozed from the gum behind his left incisor. With any luck, that was the source of the blood she'd seen on Casper. She shooed Mojo inside, then coaxed the frightened white boxer from behind the bush.

"Easy, Casper." She dabbed at the blood streaking his fur, and it came off on her fingers. He watched her with those unnervingly solemn, mismatched eyes. Other than Mojo's bloody slobber, he was unharmed.

Thank God. Cara plopped down on the grass at Casper's side, her legs rubbery, heart pounding. "You are not good for my adrenaline levels, you know that?"

Casper was going to take some work. He'd come into the shelter as a stray, and he would need time to feel comfortable again as part of a family, if he ever had been. He wasn't a mean dog, just frightened and defensive. He lay beside Cara now, head between his front paws, weary eyes glazed.

In retrospect, she shouldn't have offered treats in front of both dogs so soon. Mojo had sniffed at Casper's cookie, and Casper had defended what was his. Resource guarding wasn't unusual for a dog like Casper, who'd been on his own for a while. Cara had made a rookie mistake. She was distracted today, but that was no excuse.

Mojo whined from the other side of the door. Casper watched, his posture relaxed.

She stood and opened the back door, keeping a close eye on her troublemaking canines. Mojo trotted out, nuzzled Cara's hand, and took off across the yard in search of a ball. After a moment, Casper got to his feet and followed him. Mojo spun around him, his front legs pressed to the earth, tail up, as he invited Casper to play.

That's more like it. Cara breathed a sigh of relief. She shoved her hands into the pockets of her jeans to ward off the cold breeze as she watched them.

Mojo was a funny-looking dog with brown brindle stripes that darkened to black along his back. He had a sturdy body, full tail, and a face thicker than a full-blooded boxer. No one knew what he was mixed with, but something in his coloration and stance suggested German shepherd to Cara. No matter his heritage, he was all fun, the most laid-back, well-mannered foster she'd ever had.

After watching Mojo try in vain for several minutes to get Casper to play, she headed for the house, chilled from too long outside in only a thin jacket. The dogs bounded ahead and waited for her at the sliding glass door.

"Lead the way, Mojo," she told the brown dog. His tail beat the vinyl siding as she opened the door, then he scrambled across the kitchen to check his bowl, as if the dog food fairy might have filled it while they were playing outside. "In a little while. Let's get Casper settled in first."

Despite his emaciated appearance, Casper had been well fed at the shelter for the past three days, and she didn't want him to get sick from eating before his nervous stomach settled. Cara flipped on the gas fireplace, then led the way upstairs.

Casper tucked his tail as he followed her into the master bedroom.

"It'll be a while before we make it up here tonight, I'm afraid. It's New Year's Eve, and I'm going out. But I wanted you to see it first in the daylight. You can join Mojo and me in the big bed." She eyed his soiled fur, then grabbed an old sheet and spread it over her pink-flowered comforter. Before she went out tonight, he definitely needed a bath.

She kept talking, knowing that her calm voice and demeanor, as well as Mojo's, would put Casper more quickly at ease. She sat on the bed and patted it, inviting them up. Mojo leaped up and made himself at home, while Casper stood anxiously at her feet. She told him all about tonight's party while stroking his chin until, with a shy wag of his nub, he hopped up on her other side.

"That's a good boy." She lay back and closed her eyes, a dog on each side.

What was better than that? Maybe she'd take a quick nap before Merry arrived. Gina's funeral had left her drained.

The chiming of the doorbell sent Casper into fits of hysterical barking. He launched himself off the bed and ran a lap around the bedroom. Mojo jumped down and headed for the hall, his bark mixing with Casper's as both dogs raced downstairs.

Cara glanced at her watch as she hurried after them. Merry wasn't due for another two hours. Whoever it was had lousy timing.

She sprinted into the kitchen and grabbed a handful of peanut-butter dog biscuits from the counter.

"Come, Casper." She used the biscuits as a lure, and the dog crept into his crate, still eyeing the front door with suspicion. She rewarded him with a handful of peanut-butter yummies, then draped the crate with a thick blanket, hoping the darkness would help calm him.

The doorbell pealed again. Casper's booming bark filled the room, accompanied by the sound of his body slamming into the metal bars of the crate. So much for calm.

"Shhh," Cara whispered, then hurried toward the front door. "Coming."

Mojo stood in the hallway, tail wagging in anticipation of their visitor.

Without pausing to check the peephole, she yanked the door open, then gaped at the man standing there. He filled her doorway, tall and solid in worn jeans and a black leather jacket. Dark brown hair was pushed back from his forehead with a slight wave. His brown eyes settled on hers, and a little ping of warmth traveled through her.

"Matt Dumont. I live next door." He jerked his head toward the townhouse to the left of hers.

Cara nodded. Oh yeah, she knew who he was, and she'd been doing her best to avoid him for the past year. Well, now she had a name to put with the face formerly known as "Mr. FMH," a term she and her friend Olivia had coined back in college for a guy that was "fuck me hot." Matt sure was, not that she had any intention of acting on it.

She glanced down at herself, painfully aware of the streak of bloody slobber on her shirtsleeve and the way she was panting for breath after wrangling an uncooperative sixty-pound boxer into his crate. Of course, if they had to meet after all this time, she'd be a mess.

She pasted on the sweetest smile she could muster as Casper growled from the kitchen. "Nice to meet you. I'm Cara Medlen."

"'Bout time I knew your name, don't you think?" The corner of his mouth hitched in amusement as those cocoa eyes searched hers. He was even more handsome up close, staring at her like that, so intense she almost forgot to breathe.

"I guess so."

"So, what's the story with your dogs, Cara?"

She sucked in a breath. "What story?"

His eyes narrowed, less warm now. "You tell me."

She crossed her arms over her chest. What was it with her neighbors and their closed-mindedness about her foster dogs? "We haven't broken any rules, Mr. Dumont, so if you don't mind..."

She moved to close the front door, but he stepped forward, blocking her. "Actually, I do mind."

Cara felt the force of his stare right down to her coral-painted toenails.

"The white dog—is he receiving some kind of medical treatment?"

He was so close now she could smell the faint scent of his aftershave. Too close, but she refused to give him the satisfaction of backing away. She straightened her spine, wishing for a few more inches so she could glare at him without having to look up. "What exactly are you suggesting?"

"I can see into your backyard from my upstairs hallway." He tilted his head. "I think I know what's going on here."

Cara scrunched her nose. What in the world was he accusing her of, mowing her lawn in the wrong direction? Crap, had he been watching last week when she tripped over Mojo and fell in a pile of dog poop? She'd stripped out of her jeans right there in the backyard and run inside half naked. Her cheeks burned. "Perhaps you should be more specific."

He glanced down at the dog at her feet. Mojo sat, ears back, his shoulder against Cara's left leg. A crash echoed from the kitchen as Casper thrashed in his crate. "You fighting these dogs, Ms. Medlen?"

She couldn't help it; she snorted with laughter at the absolute absurdity of his accusation. "Are you serious?"

Matt pinned her in his laser-like gaze, looking deadly serious. "That a pit bull?"

"A boxer. Thank you for your concern, Mr. Dumont, but maybe next time you should mind your own business."

And with that, she slammed the door in his face.

Excerpt from FOR KEEPS

Love to the Rescue Book 2
Link to list of buy links: http://www.rachellacey.com/for-keeps/

Chapter One

Merry Atwater was about to do something she hadn't done in almost a decade. She closed her eyes, clasped her hands together, and prayed. As in, to God. She had little faith the Big Guy was listening, but she was desperate.

When she opened her eyes, the numbers on the screen hadn't changed. Not that she expected God to alter Triangle Boxer Rescue's account balance, but He did perform miracles from time to time, didn't He? The truth was, the animal rescue she had poured her heart and soul into for the last six years was flat broke.

"What am I going to do?" She steepled her fingers and pressed them to her mouth.

Ralph, her six-year-old boxer, scooted closer on the couch. He plopped his head into her lap and gazed up at her with adoring brown eyes. Behind him, her foster puppies Chip and Salsa lay piled on top of each other. Collectively, they took up nearly the whole couch, but Merry didn't mind. She enjoyed having a couch full of happy dogs, especially knowing she had saved each one from an uncertain future at the shelter, guaranteeing them a happy ending through Triangle Boxer Rescue.

She'd founded TBR as a twenty-two-year-old fresh out of nursing school, eager to do more to help the dogs she'd come to love and depend on. Since then, she'd devoted as much of her time and hard-earned money as she could spare to saving abandoned and abused boxers in and around the small town of Dogwood, North Carolina.

She'd been successful too, at least at first. Several years ago, she'd begun receiving an anonymous donation of one thousand dollars a month from an unknown benefactor. She'd tried and failed to find out who was behind the mysterious donations, but at some point, she'd come to depend on them. Then, six months ago, the donations had stopped. Now the rescue's bank account was drained, and she'd nearly maxed out her personal credit card trying to cover the difference.

She traced her fingers over the zigzag pattern on her pajama pants. It was nearly nine o'clock, and she was ready to call it a night. She had a twelve-hour shift ahead of her tomorrow and needed a good night's sleep.

A quiet knock sounded at her front door. Ralph lifted his head and let out a sleepy bark, while Chip and Salsa tumbled onto the floor in a tangle of puppy legs.

Merry sucked in a breath. Had God heard her prayer after all? Had someone arrived to miraculously bail Triangle Boxer Rescue out of financial ruin?

Not likely, but she'd always considered herself a glass-half-full kind of girl.

"Just a minute," she called as she herded the puppies behind the gate in the kitchen then walked to the front door with Ralph at her side. She pressed her eye to the peephole, hesitant to open the door to an unexpected guest in her pajamas.

A woman stood outside, dressed in a pink tank top and jean shorts. Wet tendrils of brown hair stuck to the sides of her face from the rain pouring beyond the safe shelter of Merry's porch. She looked vaguely familiar. A neighbor, maybe?

Merry pulled the door open. Ralph let out a powerful bark, eyes fixed on the bedraggled dog at the woman's side. It appeared to be some sort of Lab mix, with soggy amber fur and the kind of glazed eyes that Merry had seen too many times.

She gave Ralph a quick hand signal to keep him from greeting the unknown dog. He sat, tail wiggling against the hardwood floor.

"Hi," the woman said, extending a rain-drenched hand. "I'm Kelly Pointer. I live down the street." Kelly looked to the left, toward the cul-de-sac at the other end of the road.

Right. Merry had seen her before when she was out walking her dogs. She took Kelly's hand and shook. "Sure. Hi, Kelly. What can I do for you?"

"Well, I heard you rescue dogs." Kelly gestured to the dog at her feet. It stood, hunched, looking pathetic and miserable, and a heavy feeling settled in Merry's gut.

God hadn't sent an answer to her prayers. Instead, He'd added to her burden.

"Yes," she answered carefully. "I'm the director of Triangle Boxer Rescue."

She glanced pointedly at Ralph, still sitting politely at her side. He cocked his chestnut head, gazing up at their visitor with warm chocolate eyes that had melted many a heart.

"Well," Kelly said, "I found this stray. She's been wandering the neighborhood, and I was afraid she'd get hit by a car. I was hoping you could take her."

Merry looked at the stray. The rain-soaked Lab mix avoided her gaze, looking like she'd dart off into the watery darkness if given half a chance. "Have you called the Dogwood Shelter to see if anyone's looking for her?"

"Uh, no. I just brought her to you. I was hoping you could take her." Her neighbor extended a thin piece of white rope that had been fashioned into a makeshift collar and leash.

"Well, I don't exactly—" Merry gripped the rope, looking down at the pathetic dog on her front porch. This wasn't the first time someone had brought her a random dog, expecting her to take it because she worked in animal rescue, and it wouldn't be the last.

She'd always felt it a bit rude and presumptuous. It wasn't as if Kelly didn't have a home of her own where the dog could stay, warm and dry. Merry would have been happy to help her find the stray a home. But nope, she was apparently the designated receptacle for all unwanted dogs in the area, like it or not.

"Good luck with her. She seems sweet." Kelly tucked her hands into her pockets and turned to go.

"Thanks, but I'll probably have to bring her to the shelter in the morning."

Kelly's eyes rounded. "What? I thought maybe you could keep her, or something."

"I run a rescue—for boxers. This is not a boxer. I already have two fosters and a dog of my own. I really can't keep her." Merry said the words. She meant them too. Then she glanced down at the dog huddled on her front porch, and she knew she'd never follow through.

Kelly shrugged. "Well, that sucks. I hope she finds a home."

And with that, she walked off into the rainy night.

Merry looked at the dog, who, for tonight at least, was hers. "So you're spending the night with us, huh?" The soggy Lab mix stared at the floor of Merry's porch, tail tucked between her legs. She reeked like wet, dirty dog.

Merry looped the rope around the railing. "Just a minute. I'll be right back, okay?"

She stepped inside and put Ralph behind the gate in the kitchen with her two nosy foster puppies. She couldn't introduce the new dog tonight, knowing nothing about her, and, besides, she wasn't keeping her long enough for it to matter.

She'd have her scanned for a microchip, call the local shelters, and, if all else failed, she'd look for another rescue to take her, because Merry couldn't keep her. She never kept more than three.

And in case God had forgotten, Merry was broke. She'd learned a long time ago that she couldn't save them all. It was a bitter lesson to swallow, but true, and important to remember, lest she drown in guilt over the ones who couldn't be saved.

She returned to the porch with a towel and gently rubbed as much rainwater as she could from the soggy stray. "Ready to come inside?"

The dog planted her feet, unwilling to enter the house. Merry shrugged, unfazed. She sat on the top step, staring out into the rainy June night, still warm and muggy despite the hour.

"Life's been pretty crappy to you lately, huh?" she said softly. "I know what that feels like. It's going to get better, though. At least you have a dry bed waiting for you tonight, right?"

She kept talking, watching the rain fall beyond the protection of her front porch. Finally, the stray took a hesitant step toward her.

Merry reached out and stroked her chest, telling her what a good girl she was, patiently earning her trust. After a while, she stood and gave the rope a gentle tug. The dog followed her into the house.

The boxers in the kitchen barked and pranced, eager to make acquaintance with their visitor. Not yet. The dog at her side was tense, defensive. Terrified.

Merry led her to the crate she kept in the den for new dogs just getting settled.

It would do. For tonight.

* * *

T. J. Jameson leaned a hip against the counter and watched the pretty brunette's frown deepen. From the looks of it, his buddy David Johnson had just declined her credit card. David owned Dogwood Animal Hospital. T.J., on his way home after checking on a colicky horse out in Creedmoor, had stopped by to see if his friend might have a recommendation to replace the dog trainer who'd just bailed on him.

The brunette tossed back a curly lock of hair and rummaged inside her purse. She was dressed for suburbia in fitted jean shorts, a purple blouse, and sparkly flip-flops, with a brown dog at her feet. T.J. pictured her in Wranglers and cowboy boots, and he liked that image a whole lot better. Dressed like that, he'd really have a hard time taking his eyes off her.

She glanced over, and their eyes met. Hers were a bottomless hazel that sparkled with trouble.

She turned back to David. "Try this one," she said, handing over a blue credit card.

David swiped it through his card reader. "You've been paying for a lot of foster dogs with your personal card lately."

She shrugged. "This one's not technically a foster. I'm just keeping her for a day or two, to see if anyone shows up to claim her."

Behind him, the door chimed. T.J. glanced over his shoulder to see a teenager in baggy jeans and a T-shirt emblazoned with "#AWESOME" enter the waiting room, busily texting on his cell phone. A brown-and-white dog walked at his side, some kind of mixed breed. It lunged toward the one the brunette held, barking and snarling, straining against the end of its leash.

"Knock it off," the teenager said, pulling the dog toward the other end of the waiting room.

T.J.'s skin prickled. Clearly that animal was not a suitable pet. It was only a matter of time before it bit someone. He ran a hand over his throat, feeling for the scars that had long faded.

He looked back at the brunette. She'd moved her dog out of sight behind the reception desk and was signing her receipt.

"Thanks, Dr. Johnson. I'll see you next week for the puppies' next round of vaccinations." She started for the door with the brown dog at her heel.

The teenager's mutt lunged again, and this time its leash pulled free. It bounded across the lobby toward the brunette and her dog.

Vicious barking shattered the air, setting T.J.'s adrenaline pumping. The brunette froze, and the dog behind her cowered against her legs. Easy bait.

His stomach soured at the thought of her at the dog's mercy, her blood staining that pretty purple blouse as she tried to defend herself. No. No way.

"Hey!" T.J. lunged in front of the runaway dog.

It stopped and snarled at him, teeth bared. T.J. felt the hair on his arms stand on end. He raised his arms as if he were corralling a wayward calf and took a step toward the animal.

The dog pinned its ears and growled.

"Brutus, no!" The teenager grabbed the end of the leash and hauled the dog, still growling, into an open exam room.

T.J.'s heart thumped against his ribs. The scars on his neck stung, a vicious memory of the night he'd almost gotten his throat ripped out. He still heard the snarling barks, felt the teeth crushing his throat and his own warm blood flowing over his skin.

"Holy shit."

He turned his head to see the brunette staring at him, her hazel eyes wide. His hand was on her shoulder before he knew what he was doing. "Are you okay?"

She nodded. "You are so lucky you didn't get bit just now."

Yeah, he knew that; knew it better than most. He pulled back, tucking his thumbs through his belt loops. "Better me than you."

"He wasn't really after me; he was after my dog. But I was ready for him." She opened her right hand to reveal a small, black spray canister.

T.J.'s eyebrows lifted. "Mace?"

"Citronella spray. It's kind of like Mace for dogs, except it doesn't hurt them." She slid the can into her purse. "FYI, next time you might not want to wave your arms around in an aggressive dog's face. It's asking for trouble, but...thanks. Most people wouldn't bother to try. You're our hero."

She gave him a sweet smile, then strode out the front door, brown dog trotting along at her side.

T.J. stared, then snapped his mouth shut, feeling more confused than heroic. He turned to David, who still stood behind the reception desk, flipping through paperwork. "Who was that?"

David waggled his bushy eyebrows with a smile. "Merry Atwater. She's a nurse, so at least she could have patched you up if you'd needed it."

T.J. grunted. Good to know. "That kid with the vicious dog is a client of yours?"

"His father is, but he's out of town. Brutus isn't all bad, but the family refuses to have him neutered, and he gets a little territorial around female dogs."

"Brutus? The dog's name is Brutus? That should be a warning right there." T.J. had never had a dog, never planned on getting one, but if he did, he'd find a reputable breeder, choose one with champion bloodlines and a solid temperament. He'd never understood why people took in dogs like that one, dogs of unknown heritage, with obvious behavioral problems.

He'd seen what happened when dogs like that got loose. He'd seen livestock attacked by prowling dogs. Hell, he'd come within an inch of losing his own life to a couple of stray mutts. Dogs like Brutus were a serious problem.

David nodded. "Brutus might need to be muzzled in the lobby area. I'll have a talk with them about it. So what brings you out my way?"

"Hoping you might be able to help me out."

David headed for the back room, motioning for T.J. to follow. "Oh yeah, how's that?"

"That dog trainer I hired for the summer camp bailed on me." He was seriously pissed about it too. He'd spent months getting everything in place, and now, with only a week to go, he was back at square one.

"So just put the kids to work in the barn," his friend said with a shrug.

"I plan to, but dogs are an important part of the camp—for Noah especially." And the whole point of the camp was to help his nephew. Noah had been diagnosed a few years ago as a child with high-functioning autism. He was a smart kid, bright as a hundred-watt bulb, but he struggled to communicate with his peers, which had led to problems at school.

T.J.'s sister Amy was a single mom fighting to make ends meet. She wouldn't accept money from him, no matter how hard he tried to help. Instead, he'd decided to establish a summer camp on his farm to help kids like his nephew, using his horses for equine therapy and incorporating a local dog trainer who'd bring several trained therapy dogs to work with the kids.

Noah communicated with dogs on a level he struggled to achieve with members of his own species. The camp absolutely couldn't happen without dogs.

"Well, here's an idea." David reached into a wire crate to check the IV port on a chocolate-colored cocker spaniel. "Merry Atwater, the lady who just left? She runs a boxer rescue, and I happen to remember one of her dogs is a certified therapy dog. Maybe she could help you out."

"Really?" T.J. thought back to the pretty brunette. He couldn't quite picture her getting her perfectly manicured hands dirty out on his farm.

David nodded. "She's good people. And between you and me, her rescue's in some financial trouble right now. If you offered her a donation in return for her help, I'm sure she'd be more than happy to be part of your camp."

"I don't know. She didn't really look like the farm type to me." The last thing he needed was some girly-girl running around on his farm, complaining about getting her expensive shoes dirty or breaking a fingernail.

But camp started next week, and, at the moment, he had no other leads.

"She's tougher than she looks." David led the way back to the waiting room, where he pulled a business card from a pile in a drawer behind the reception desk. "Give her a call. See what she says."

* * *

Merry pursed her lips and tried to ignore the dog sulking in the crate at the far end of the kitchen. She'd called every shelter in the area to report her found, but so far, no owner had come forward. From the looks of her, the mutt probably hadn't had an owner in some time. Her fur was matted with burs and mud, her nails untrimmed, ribs protruding beneath her heavy coat.

Merry couldn't bring herself to take her to the shelter, but she couldn't keep her, either. She wasn't a boxer, for one thing. Not to mention, her tiny house was already at capacity with Ralph, Chip, and Salsa. And she was broke.

Couldn't forget that part.

Which led her back to the email on her screen. A woman named Tracy Jameson had emailed her, said she'd gotten Merry's name from her vet, David Johnson. She was looking for someone to help out with canine-assisted therapy at a summer camp she was running for local kids. In exchange, she'd write a check for a thousand dollars to Triangle Boxer Rescue.

Tempting. Very tempting.

Ralph was a therapy dog. Merry took him in once a week to visit the kids on the pediatric floor of Dogwood Hospital. He'd be great for the summer camp.

In fact, he'd love it a lot more than she would. To Merry, summer camp sounded dirty, sweaty, and exhausting. And while she did have some vacation time saved up at the hospital, she'd planned to spend it fund-raising for Triangle Boxer Rescue, not wilting in the summer heat on this woman's farm.

Still, a thousand dollars sounded pretty irresistible right now.

First things first. She had to figure out what to do with the stray dog in her kitchen. Merry approached the crate and eyed the nameless, hopeless dog. "So, I was thinking about putting up some flyers around the neighborhood. Want to come with me?"

The dog looked up, her brown eyes so sad, so empty, that Merry's heart broke. No matter what, this dog couldn't go to the shelter. She wouldn't last a week.

Merry opened the crate and coaxed the frightened dog out. She reached into the cabinet and pulled out a bag of training treats, then sat on the floor and praised and rewarded her for every shy wag of her tail.

Once No-Name had received a much-needed boost to her self-esteem, Merry clipped a leash onto her collar. She grabbed the pile of flyers she'd printed earlier, along with a stapler, and she was ready to go.

"You need a name," Merry told her. She named new fosters all the time, and yet she couldn't bring herself to name this one.

The dog stood patiently beside her while she stapled flyers to lampposts up and down her street and around the neighborhood. It wasn't likely, but it was possible there was a family out there somewhere looking for her and wanting her back.

No-Name stared straight ahead as they walked, making no eye contact with Merry, showing no emotion at all. Her tail hung limply behind her, which was a step up from tucked between her legs, but no amount of sweet talk from Merry could get it to wag again.

A high-pitched shriek was their only warning before a toddler barreled onto the sidewalk, arms outstretched. "Doggy! Doggy!"

Merry tightened her grip on No-Name's leash and tried to put herself between the dog and the runaway child, but it was too late. The little girl flung her arms around No-Name's neck with a squeal of glee.

"Violet!" A woman ran down the driveway after the wayward child. "Oh, my gosh."

Merry tensed, ready to intervene if necessary, but No-Name's tail wagged steadily. She looked calm. Happy even.

"Thank goodness your dog likes kids," the girl's mother said.

That was an understatement. Merry wouldn't have intentionally introduced such a new dog to anyone's child just yet, but now that it had happened, No-Name did indeed seem thrilled.

The little girl patted her roughly on the head then ran off toward a pink tricycle outside the garage. Her mom waved and followed her up the driveway. No-Name gazed after the toddler, tail still wagging.

Merry hustled her home. As they walked in the front door, her cell phone rang. She glanced at the display. "Hey, Liv."

"Hi," Olivia said. "I got your message, and no, I can't take another dog right now. I nearly got evicted from my apartment when I was fostering those damn puppies."

"Oh, come on, please? This one's full grown. She's housebroken, and I haven't even heard her bark. She'd be easy."

"Nope, sorry." Olivia Bennett had never formally agreed to foster for Triangle Boxer Rescue. She was a friend of Cara Medlen, who'd moved to Massachusetts a few months ago, leaving Merry short a good foster home, and a best friend, both of which roles Olivia had temporarily stepped in to fill.

"Know anyone looking for a dog? She's some kind of Lab mix, very shy, but well behaved."

"I'll ask around, but offhand...no."

"Okay, well, thanks anyway." Merry led the dog back into her kitchen. This morning she'd allowed her to make introductions with Ralph, and it had gone well. No-Name had tucked her tail and bowed her head submissively when Ralph greeted her. It was a good start, but she wasn't ready to throw her somewhat less predictable foster puppies into the mix just yet.

Currently, they were asleep upstairs in her bedroom. If No-Name stayed much longer, she'd think about introducing them all, but she hoped she'd be passing her along before that became necessary.

She opened her laptop to see if any of the Lab or all-breed rescues had responded. They hadn't, but the email from Tracy Jameson still waited in her inbox.

She didn't want to get involved in a summer camp, but maybe...

Maybe she could make it work to her advantage. She sent Tracy a quick reply, asking to meet with her to discuss things further, then closed her laptop to start preparing dinner for herself and the dogs.

The next day, she worked her usual twelve-hour shift at Dogwood Hospital. Exhausted, she grabbed a Cajun Filet Biscuit from the Bojangles' drive-through and headed for Tracy's farm.

Like many towns in the area, Dogwood had experienced a burst of growth in the past decade due to its proximity to the Research Triangle Park, where many large pharmaceutical and other high-tech companies were located. Modern neighborhoods gradually gave way to rolling country roads that hadn't changed in generations.

She drove down one of these country roads, past the rusted-out shell of a barn, a corn field, and several miles of open farmland. Merry rolled down her window and breathed in the fresh air. She loved to drive through the country, see the horses and cows, smell the wheat and fresh earth. Actually rolling up her sleeves and getting dirty didn't sound as appealing, but if it would help the rescue, she'd take one for the team.

Tracy's farm was at the end of the street, a modest two-story, brick-front ranch house. Tracy had texted her a few minutes ago to say she was running late, so Merry pulled past the house and parked by the barn to finish her chicken biscuit. It melted in her mouth in buttery perfection. She washed it down with sweet tea and a sigh of contentment.

Behind the barn, two horses grazed in a lush green field, while a third lounged nearby beneath a shade tree. Merry's knowledge of horses was pretty much confined to the pages of Black Beauty (which had earned her a childhood nickname of Merrylegs), but these were obviously well cared for and absolutely gorgeous. Their brown coats glistened in the sun over sleek, well-muscled haunches.

She leaned back in her seat and settled in to watch them. The larger horse, a male, swooshed his tail to and fro, fly-swatting for himself and the female beside him. Equine chivalry. Aww.

A few minutes later, a black Ford F-350 pickup truck pulled into the driveway with a roar of its diesel engine and parked next to Merry's CR-V. She looked up, impressed. That was a badass truck for a chick.

She stepped out of her SUV, making sure she wasn't wearing any crumbs on her scrubs, and rounded the rear bumper just as the driver's door opened on the truck.

She saw the cowboy boots first, brown-stitched leather at least a man's size twelve. Her gaze traveled up a pair of jeans filled out by very muscular, very masculine legs. The man wearing them swung out of the cab and tipped his cowboy hat at her.

Well, well. It was her would-be hero from Dr. Johnson's office. What in the world was he doing here?

She'd never been a big fan of cowboys, but this guy was seriously sexy. His dark hair was mostly hidden by the hat, which shadowed his face, hiding the exact shade of the brown eyes currently locked on hers. He wore a crisp, blue T-shirt tucked into his jeans, filled to perfection by strong, muscled man.

His face was rugged, a bit too rough to grace the cover of a catalog for western wear, but good God, he was gorgeous. And clearly not Tracy Jameson.

"Merry Atwater?" His voice matched his image perfectly, deep and smooth.

"That's me. And you are?"

He extended a hand. "T.J. Jameson. Thanks for driving all the way out here. I figured you'd like to see the place before you made up your mind."

She took his hand and shook. "Uh, where's Tracy?"

His lips curved in amusement. "Tracy Allan Jameson III, in the flesh. My granddaddy was Tracy, Dad calls himself Trace, I go by T.J."

She almost swallowed her tongue. "You're Tracy."

"Yes, ma'am, but please call me T.J."

Merry sucked in a breath. So Tracy Jameson was a guy. And not just any guy, but a strappingly handsome cowboy oozing testosterone from every pore.

Summer camp had just gotten much hotter, in a completely new way.

Excerpt from EVER AFTER

Love to the Rescue Book 3
Link to list of buy links: http://www.rachellacey.com/ever-after/

Chapter One

Red paint dripped from Olivia Bennett's fingers. She tightened her grip on the metal canister in her right hand and gave it a solid shake. Beneath her feet, the ladder wobbled. With a startled squeak, she sent a burst of spray paint onto her boots.

"Sorry, Liv," Terence called from below.

"Watch it, will you?" She pressed her palm against the cool, corrugated metal of the factory wall and took a deep breath. Then she lifted her right hand and pressed the valve on the spray paint canister, forming a brilliantly red "S" on the side of the building.

"Almost done," Kristi said.

Easy for her to say, standing safely on the ground next to Terence. At the top of the ladder, Olivia fought to keep her balance as the remnants of several margaritas sloshed in her stomach. Hell of a way to end her twenty-ninth birthday.

The beam of Kristi's flashlight cast Olivia's shadow in stark silhouette over her red-painted message. She leaned right to spray another "S" but couldn't reach. She'd have to come down and move the ladder to continue, but a muffled sound captured her attention.

Mew.

The sound was soft yet keening. A kitten? Some other baby animal? She craned her head, peering into the darkness. "Did you guys hear that?"

"Hear what?" Terence asked, his tone wary.

"It sounded like a kitten."

Kristi panned the flashlight around them, plunging Olivia into darkness. She leaned a hip against the side of the building to steady herself.

"I don't see anything," Kristi said.

"Okay, put that light back on me so I can get down."

The flashlight's beam once more illuminated her, and Olivia scrambled quickly to solid ground. "I heard some kind of little animal crying while I was up there, so keep an eye out."

"Will do." Terence moved the ladder over so that she could reach the next section of wall to be painted and held it steady as she climbed back up.

Six letters to go, and they were out of here. Terence would drive them to his place for a post-graffiti celebration. Olivia was in no condition to drive herself anywhere tonight. Adrenaline mixed with trepidation as she stood at the top of the ladder yet again. The margarita buzz had faded enough to know she was doing a crazy, stupid thing that wasn't going to do a damn thing to help the chickens who arrived here daily, their only hope that death would be quick and merciful.

Based on what the undercover cameras had captured, that hope was slim.

She ground her teeth, her fingers clenched around the spray can. It was inhumane the way those birds were treated. Actually, it was inhumane the way most factory-farmed animals were treated, but this was happening right here in her little hometown of Dogwood, North Carolina.

Mew.

A flash of white fur caught her eye, disappearing into the bushes behind the factory. If it was a kitten, it was tiny. Was its mother nearby? There weren't any houses for miles around. Dammit. Now she was going to have to go on a kitten hunt before she went home. She couldn't leave it out here to fend for itself.

"Hurry up, Liv," Kristi called from below her.

Olivia raised the canister and let loose another blast of red paint. She'd just started "I" when the sound of an approaching vehicle reached her. Her finger slipped, and a fresh coat of paint soaked her hands.

Kristi and Terence must have heard it too, because the flashlight shut off, leaving her at the top of the ladder in pitch darkness, afraid to move. Headlights slashed through the night from Garrett Road, some two hundred feet to her left. They slowed, then tires crunched over gravel as the car turned into the factory parking lot.

Christ on a cracker.

"Get the hell down, Liv. We've got to get out of here!" Terence whispered.

A swirl of blue lights turned the night into a kaleidoscope of oh, shit. She pressed against the side of the building, stymied by paint-slickened fingers as she fumbled for the top of the ladder.

She was so not getting arrested on her birthday.

Except that she so was. A spotlight shone from the cruiser, illuminating her in a blaze of light so bright she could do nothing but press a hand over her eyes and count how many ways spray-painting Halverson Foods's chicken-processing plant had been a bad idea.

The ladder shifted beneath her, and she groped for the top rung. The combination of the spinning blue lights with the piercing glare of the spotlight was seriously disorienting.

"Hands where I can see them," a male voice boomed.

She shoved her hands into the air, managing to smack herself in the face with the can of spray paint in the process. It fell to the ground with a muffled thump. Oh, this sucked.

"Come down from the ladder, nice and slow, and keep those hands up," the cop instructed. He sounded nice-ish. Maybe he'd go easy on her. Maybe...

Awkwardly, she fumbled with her right foot for the next rung of the ladder. It swayed dangerously to the side. "Terence!" she hissed, her fingernails scoring metal as she tried to steady herself.

Silence. She looked down, but the spotlight's glare blinded her, preventing her from seeing past her own paint-spattered boots. "Terence? Kristi?"

She managed to get her foot settled onto the rung and took a step down. No answer came from her friends. What the hell?

She lifted her left foot to take the next step, and the ladder just dropped out from beneath her. One second it was there, the next she was plummeting through space.

"Oomph," came a masculine grunt, as she slammed into someone's chest and big, strong arms closed around her.

"Terence?" Her voice was a squeak, because Terence was nowhere near this strong, and he didn't smell as good either. This man smelled faintly of cinnamon, his arms solid as steel behind her thighs, and based on the hard bulge stabbing into her kidney, he was also armed.

Oh, crap. Crap. Crap!

"Sorry," he answered her question, setting her roughly on the ground. "Not Terence."

"Oh." She staggered, still blinded by the spotlight aimed at her. Disoriented, she turned her back and blinked at her shadow on the factory's gray wall. Terence and Kristi had deserted her. Bastards.

"Keep those hands where I can see them," Invisible Cop said.

With a sigh, she placed them on the wall before her. Her hands glistened blood-red in the harsh light. She had been caught red-handed. Dammit. She'd always hated being a cliché.

* * *

Deputy Pete Sampson reached for his cuffs. When he'd taken the call about a trespasser on Halverson Foods's property, he surely hadn't expected to find a teenage girl on a ladder, covered from head to foot in red spray paint. "You want to tell me what you're doing out here tonight?"

She kept her back to him. "It's fairly obvious, right?"

He looked up. The side of the building dripped with big, red letters. It was obvious all right, but he wouldn't be surprised if she tried to talk her way out of it anyway.

"Chicken ass?" he read. What the hell was that even supposed to mean? Kids these days. He shook his head in annoyance.

She made a choking sound, squinting up at her handiwork. "I wasn't finished."

"Do tell."

"It was supposed to say Chicken Assassins."

"Ah. Well I suppose you know this is private property."

She nodded, her shoulders slumping.

"What's your name?" he asked.

"Olivia Bennett."

"I have some bad news, Olivia. You are under arrest for trespassing and vandalism. You have the right to remain silent." Pete snapped cuffs around her slender wrists as he read her her rights. He could spare her a pat-down because there was no way in hell she had anything concealed beneath that purple tank top or the fitted jeans that hugged her willowy frame.

"It's my birthday," she mumbled.

"Sorry, kid. The law makes no exception for birthdays."

"Kid?" She turned to face him, and he saw he'd been wrong about one thing. She was no teenager pulling a back-to-school prank. This woman was mid-twenties, easily, and far too beautiful to be doing what he'd just caught her doing. Her long, blond hair was pulled back in a messy ponytail, and she stared at him from wounded brown eyes.

He shrugged. "Seemed a pretty juvenile thing to do."

Chicken Assassins. In retrospect, he realized he was dealing with an animal rights activist instead of a teenaged troublemaker.

"Do you have any idea what happens to the birds in there?" she asked, her eyes bright with emotion.

"They get slaughtered." He took her elbow and guided her toward his cruiser. Her breath smelled of alcohol. "You drive out here?"

She glanced over at the red Prius parked behind the building. "Um—"

"You're drunk."

"I wouldn't say drunk, exactly." She ducked her head as he tucked her into the back of the cruiser.

"Let's find out, shall we?" He took his portable breathalyzer out of the car and crouched beside her.

Her eyes widened. "Let's not. I know my rights, deputy."

Pete stood. Great. A drunk troublemaker who knew the law. He had zero tolerance for people who drove under the influence. He'd seen firsthand the damage they inflicted on society, the lives and families torn apart.

Zach Hill had been left without a father.

Pete's gut soured. "Fine. You'll take it back at the station. Where are your keys?"

Her brows creased, and she glanced at the empty seat beside her. "I must have dropped them."

She was lying. But why? He closed the cruiser door and walked back to the building, shining his flashlight over the gravel lot. No sign of car keys. He walked to the Prius and tried the door. Locked. No keys visible inside.

She'd been looking for someone when she fell off the ladder. Maybe she'd had an accomplice. He returned to the cruiser and opened the back door. "Who's Terence?"

"A friend." She studied her shoes.

"Was he out here with you tonight?"

She shook her head. "No, sir. Just me."

But he'd seen the flicker of truth in her eyes. She'd had an accomplice all right, probably a boyfriend, since she was protecting him. "That's unfortunate, you being out here alone and intoxicated. Judge might be inclined to think you drove drunk."

"I didn't—" She pressed her lips together and looked away.

Well fine, if that was the way she wanted to play it. He buckled her in and slid behind the wheel. Fifteen minutes later, he marched her into the Dogwood County Detention Center. Olivia kept her chin up while she was fingerprinted and photographed. She blew a .078 on the breathalyzer, which meant she had almost certainly been over the limit if she had driven herself out to that factory earlier tonight.

Pete wanted to know more about this Terence she was covering for. But for now, he was ready to let her sit and think over her foolish behavior for a little while.

"Judge Gonzalez will hear your case first thing in the morning," he told her, as he led her down the hall to the holding pen. Lucky for her, she was the department's only visitor tonight. "You got someone to come bail you out?"

"What?" She eyed the cell with its steel bench, toilet, and sink, her eyes wide and horrified.

"You've been arrested, Miss Bennett. Now you need to call someone to bail you out."

"Um, right now? It's like one o'clock in the morning."

He shrugged, fighting a smile at the incredulous look on her face. "You break the law in the middle of the night, you either rouse someone from bed to bail you out or you bunk with us."

She gripped his wrist as he propelled her inside the holding cell. "Wait! Okay, yes. I need to make a phone call."

"All right." He took her by the elbow and steered her down the hall to the phone.

"Could you?" She held out her cuffed hands. "Please?"

"Fine." He uncuffed her and sat on the bench against the wall while she made her call.

She stood there, looking forlorn and vulnerable for several long seconds, then shook her head and picked up the phone. He'd expected her to dial the boyfriend she'd been looking for earlier, but instead she called someone named Merry.

"It's Olivia. I'm sorry to bother you this late, but I didn't know who else to call."

Pete tossed an arm over the back of the bench and watched her. Olivia kept her back to him, her shoulders hunched. Her friend apparently hadn't picked up, as she left a message and ended the call.

"No luck?" he asked.

She kept her back turned. "Can I try someone else?"

"Go ahead." He watched as she dialed another number. She spoke in hushed tones, then hung up and rested her forehead against the wall.

He stood. "All right then."

She turned those wounded eyes on him again as he led her back down the hall to the holding cell.

He slammed the cell door behind her with a solid clang for effect. "Make yourself comfortable. We'll let you know if anyone shows up to bail you out."

And with a chuckle at her expression, he left her there.

* * *

What a jerk.

Olivia adjusted her head against the metal bench. He might be handsome as hell, but Deputy Sampson had looked downright gleeful when he'd locked her up, and that was just rude. Now she'd spent the night in jail, and oh, how it had sucked. Thank goodness she'd sweet-talked the young guy behind the desk into letting her use the ladies' room down the hall, because that toilet...

She eyed it with disgust. God help her if Deputy Hot Stuff were to come back and catch her with her pants down. No way. She'd sooner wet her pants. Almost.

"Ugh," she groaned out loud. Her head throbbed, and her back ached. Spray-painting the Halverson Foods chicken-processing plant was officially her worst idea ever. And assuming she got her ass bailed out of here before lunchtime, she was scheduled to work the afternoon shift at the Main Street Café.

Yep, she had learned her lesson. Big time. No more breaking the law. She just needed to get out of here and find a way to put this whole thing behind her.

"Mornin' sunshine," came a low, male voice.

She squinted up at Deputy Hot Stuff himself and...ah, Jesus, her head.

"Sleep well?" he asked, as the cell door clanged open.

"Just peachy." She sat up and rubbed her eyes.

He set two aspirin and a paper cup filled with water beside her.

"Oh, my God, thank you. I take back all the awful things I thought about you last night." She swallowed the aspirin and gulped the water greedily.

"Awful things, huh?" He didn't look like he'd been home—or slept—since last night either. His cheeks had darkened with stubble, and his eyes were weary.

"All forgotten." She leaned her head against the wall and looked at him. It hurt to focus her eyes, but no, her perception hadn't been altered by the margaritas. Deputy Sampson was one fine-looking officer of the law.

He stood tall and strong with olive skin, brown hair cut short and neat, and eyes as dark as coal. If he hadn't been the one to throw her in jail, she'd have definitely tried to get his number—or rather, get him to ask for hers.

He stepped back and motioned her to follow. She stifled another groan as she stood. Every bone and muscle in her body ached. And her head felt like someone was in there with an ice pick chiseling away at the backs of her eyes.

She gazed longingly at the ladies' room as he guided her down the hall, and he stopped with a sigh.

"Go on. Five minutes to freshen up. Don't make me wait."

"Thank you," she whispered, and darted inside. She made quick use of the facilities, then splashed cold water on her face and rinsed out her mouth. It wasn't much, but she felt slightly rejuvenated when she rejoined him in the hall.

He led her next door to the courthouse but stopped her outside the courtroom. He turned those ebony eyes on hers. "Let's get one thing clear before we go in there. I can't charge you with DUI since I didn't catch you behind the wheel, but unless you want to tell me who was out there with you last night, I'm left to assume you drove yourself. You ever have to walk up to someone's front door and tell them their loved one is dead? Killed by a drunk driver?"

Jesus Christ. "No."

"If I ever catch you driving under the influence, I will throw the book at you. Are we clear?"

Also by Rachel Lacey

Risking It All Series

Rock With You
Run to You
Crazy For You
Can't Forget You

About the Author

Rachel Lacey is a contemporary romance author and semi-reformed travel junkie. She's been climbed by a monkey on a mountain in Japan, gone scuba diving on the Great Barrier Reef, and camped out overnight in New York City for a chance to be an extra in a movie. These days, the majority of her adventures take place on the pages of the books she writes. She lives in warm and sunny North Carolina with her husband, son, and a variety of rescue pets.

Rachel loves to keep in touch with her readers! You can find her at:

RachelLacey.com
Twitter @rachelslacey
Facebook.com/RachelLaceyAuthor

46240144R00087

Made in the USA
Middletown, DE
27 July 2017

Amy motioned for Luke to follow her into the living room. "You really don't need to stay. I appreciate you fixing the internet for us, but—"

"I want to stay," he said. "If it's okay with you, of course."

She sighed. "This is silly. You know that, right? We don't know each other anymore, Luke."

"I think you're wrong." He gave her a wicked smile, which proved his point because it set her heart racing. Then he proceeded to make small talk with her until Noah had finished his homework. When Noah hooked up her laptop and streamed the latest Brick Tricks video to the TV, Luke sat next to him on the couch and watched it with him.

All thirty minutes of it.

They talked about Legos, and, when the video ended, Noah took Luke to his bedroom to show him his Lego collection. When Amy peeked in fifteen minutes later to see what was taking them so long, she found Luke sitting on the floor beside Noah, building a Lego tree house like the one they'd just watched on YouTube.

It made her feel all warm and mushy inside to see them sitting there like that. Noah rarely bonded with people so quickly, especially men. She'd often worried over how the lack of a father figure would impact his life. Granted, his Uncle T.J. provided him with a solid male role model, but was it enough?

Luke looked up at her, and she gave him a look that she hoped he understood meant that it was time for him to leave. No sense getting Noah used to having him around when he was only in town for the wedding.

Apparently able to take a hint, Luke turned to Noah, "I've got to get going. I promised my mom I'd be home in time to help her with supper, and I can't break a promise, especially not to my mom. You know how it is, right?"

Noah nodded. "You can come watch Brick Tricks with me again sometime if you want."

"I'd like that. I'll probably be around a lot for the next week and a half helping your mom get this place ready for the wedding." He stood and crossed the room to Amy.

"I still can't quite believe I agreed to let them get married here." The ramifications of that decision just kept amplifying in her mind. Good God, there was so much to get done.

"Don't worry about it. Joe's been on the phone all day, rustling up help. As long as you don't mind having a bunch of people out here pitching in, we'll pretty much take care of everything."

"What about when I'm at work?"

"You don't even have to give us a key. We can just work out back when you're not home."

She sighed. "That's silly. I trust you."

He smiled, and it made her insides feel all warm and shivery. She shouldn't be thinking about giving Luke a key to her house. Because...

Well, because she still wanted him.

And she knew better than to fall for him a second time.

* * *

Luke spent the better part of Wednesday ripping out the carpet in Amy's living room. The hardwoods beneath had seen better days, but once they'd been sanded and stained, they should look good as new. Amy's little dog watched him from the couch, which currently resided in the kitchen.

Out back, Joe's friend Max rode his lawnmower back and forth across the field, taming years of overgrowth.

"You know, I don't think I ever asked what your name is," Luke said to the dog.

It just watched him.

"It's Yoda," Amy said from behind him.

Luke looked over his shoulder at her and smiled. Between his work and the roar of the mower out back, he hadn't heard her come in. "Cute."

"Noah named him."

"I figured." He stood to face her.

Amy walked over to check out his progress. "Wow. It looks so much better already."

"Yeah, that carpet needed to go. Had to have been thirty years old."

"Older probably." She bent and yanked at the next section of carpet, but he hadn't removed the nails yet, so it wasn't going anywhere. Her fingers slipped, and she stumbled backward, her ass landing flush against his groin.

His dick hardened at the contact. He put his hands on her shoulders to steady her. "You alright?"

She spun to face him, eyes wide, lips parted. They stood like that for several long seconds while lust thickened in the air around them. His heart thumped a hard rhythm against his ribs, every cell in his body attuned to the woman in his arms.

"Amy." His voice was a low rumble. "Tell me now if you don't want me to kiss you."

She sucked in a breath, her gaze dipping to his lips.

He slid his hands from her shoulders to her waist, then dipped his head and brushed his lips against hers. And *damn.* Just that simple contact made him weak at the knees. Her lips parted beneath his, deepening the kiss. His tongue brushed hers, and he felt a shiver ripple through her body.

God, she tasted good. Like teenaged fantasies and moonlit nights on a blanket beneath the stars.

"Amy," he whispered, drawing her closer against him. His hands roamed her body, familiarizing themselves with her new curves. She whimpered, her head falling back as he nibbled at that sensitive spot on her neck that had always driven her completely wild.

"No fair," she said hoarsely. "You're cheating."

He swirled his tongue over her skin, and she gasped, her hips thrusting against his. "Not cheating," he murmured. "I studied hard to learn what you like."

"Luke—" She planted her hands on his chest and looked at him. "This is a bad idea."

He grinned at her. "Are you sure? Because I thought it was the best idea I'd had all day."

"We can't—we shouldn't—" Her pupils were wide, her cheeks flushed.

And it made him want to fuck her until she'd forgotten her name. It would be even better now than it had been when they were teenagers, and it had been pretty fucking great even then. "Okay," he said instead. He dropped his arms to his sides, noticing with some satisfaction that she looked as disappointed as he felt. "But just out of curiosity, why not?"

She looked away. "Well, for starters, there's our history together."

"Pretty great history as I remember it. And you know what they say about history repeating itself."

Amy glared at him.